Dancing Max Hits Guadalcanal
or
When in Doubt, Rhumba

Dancing Max Hits Guadalcanal
or
When in Doubt, Rhumba

A Max Royster Mystery

by Frank Hickey

Dancing Max Hits Guadalcanal, or, When In Doubt, Rhumba

A Max Royster Mystery

by Frank Hickey
A Max Royster Mystery

Copyright © 2019 by Frank Hickey

Library of Congress
Catalogue-in-Publication Data

Dancing Max Hits Guadalcanal, or, When In Doubt, Rhumba
Frank Hickey
1. Fiction – Crime 2. Fiction – Mystery 3. Fiction – Hardboiled

Published by Pigtown Books

ISBN: 978-0-9970719-8-6

For further information, please contact: http://frankhickey.net

10 9 8 7 6 5 4 3 2 1

First Edition / First Issue

Dedicated to
Thomas J. Lavin, Sr., of my extended family,
First US Marine Raider Battalion,
South Pacific, 1942, amid 33% casualties.
And to all US Marines who fought on Guadalcanal Island.

CHAPTER ONE

Dancing Max Takes a Trip
or
Kidnap

"Dancing is magic," I told my class in the boathouse perched near Manhattan's East River. "Here's proof. Yesterday, I was Max Royster. Today, I legit changed my name to Dancing Max Royster."

"HURRAY!" my class hollered.

"The boathouse owner and I want a civilized genteel alcove here," I said. "Like our parents used to have. Like my generation abolished in our hippie years."

We all danced.

"Max, we interrupt this program," a man's voice boomed from the door.

"Jymmy! Catch you a partner."

"I'm catchin' you," Jymmy said. Black, burly and with missing front and side teeth, he grinned like a little boy, over a hard round belly. "Saddle up. Max, who can take over your class?"

"Can't just leave."

"You gotta."

"Why?"

"Can't say right now."

My breath went out.

"How important could it be?" I asked.

Jymmy's smile faded. Lines cut down to his mouth, making him look older.

"Someone could die," he murmured.

No dancer could hear him, over the music.

Jymmy never lied.

"Zigmund, please take my class?" I asked a handsome Polish gigolo.

"Sure," he said.

"Score a new client that way."

"If I remember right, you always got your passport on y'all, right?" Jymmy asked. "That big ugly wallet."

"Safer on my hip than in my crib," I said.

"Okay, then. Let's went."

Jymmy led me out of the boathouse and down onto a sliver of sand alongside it.

Manhattan still held slim beaches like this, at low tide. On warm days, locals would carry folding chairs and umbrellas to craft sunny afternoons here.

A motorboat with two crewmen floated on the river. They beached her on the sand. Jymmy and I climbed aboard.

"We commuting to Atlantis?" I asked.

"Supposed to be a surprise," Jymmy said.

"See that plane out there?"

A seaplane painted Prussian blue bobbed on the river.

We boated to it. Jymmy tossed me a hug and the propeller started to dance like my students ashore.

"South," the wispy blond pilot said, chewing his gum. "We goin' South."

We lifted off high above the concrete Manhattan forest. Below, Jymmy and the motorboat got smaller.

"When in doubt, steal a nap," I mumbled. "Royster's Rule."

It felt like I was pinwheeling over the globe. The seaplane heeled. So did my body. It sprawled and then slept, the miracle of every day.

"Here," the pilot said.

His voice woke me. Now the sky bloomed in a riot of blue and fat cotton clouds as we banked over a shoreline.

The plane crested down onto a calm flat sea alongside an island.

"Devil's Island?" I asked.

"Kiawah Island, South Carolina."

A tomato-red motor launch brought me to a floating dock. Waiting on the dock was a slim woman in a white Panama hat, wide sunglasses and a dark blue clinging dress.

"Max?" she asked.

Shock numbed me. I shook.

She was Diana Calia, my lover of twenty-two years ago, looking more lovely now than before.

"Why?" I managed to croak.

"May we talk? I've missed you, Max."

Sometime that night, we woke up naked and she held me. Her auburn hair, prized blue eyes and high cheekbones dazzled me like they used to.

"I should have married you," she breathed out. "Not Walter. All Walter really wanted was a mommy. He made divorce a relief."

"Me marrying you might have lasted a year," I said.

"Maybe."

"Stay with me here on Kiawah?" she asked.

"Why?" I asked. "What do you want?"

"My daughter Rua loves archaeology. She's majoring in it at Middlebury. Interning at a dig on Guadalcanal. That's in the Solomon Islands, in the South Pacific. Three days ago, in the jungle, someone kidnapped her. State Department thinks it was a radical fundamentalist group. Nobody knows nothing."

"Any ransom?"

"Not yet. Can you go there and try to get her back?"

"Me? A jungle fighter? Aged sixty-five and forty pounds too fat? Dancing Max, a student of the cocktail? Diana, with your cash and contacts, you can hire private kidnap experts. They learned how in the FBI or Army. Serve international corporations whenever a CEO gets kidnapped. Work with foreign police. They can carry guns and got clout. I got nothing like that. I'd wind up getting someone killed. Maybe me. Maybe Rua."

"Like you say, I'm shopping those outfits," she said. Her blue eyes heated. "My old editor at the *Daily News* is looking. But I need someone whom I can trust. Money doesn't buy that."

"It buys everything else."

"I'll give you $100,000 to get Rua back safely. And a home here."

"Diana, you're trying to sell me a dream. Seduce some private commando joker to find Rua. And trust him. Why would you trust me?"

"Because Rua is your daughter."

CHAPTER TWO

Jungle Daddy
or
Not Me

"You're trying to force me," I said.

Emotions croaked my voice.

Everything felt like it was spinning.

"Why're you calling me a liar?" she asked.

"D'you know what this means to me."

"Let's belay the _Falconcrest_ soap opera routine."

"Look here," she said. "Read this."

"You _Daily News_ reporters always got paper to back up your claims."

"You've been out of touch. I retired as an editor. From _The New York Times_."

"Those pieces that you wrote about me and my friends, the Playpen Irregulars, solving murders prolly helped you climb that ladder to editor heaven."

"You and your tree-house club kids who never grew up didn't help me. I helped me. Let's get that straight right now."

"Ladder, ladder."

"Just read what the lab said."

"Looks from this that Walter was not the daddy."

"No. You are."

"Assuming that I am, I still can't go humping through the rainforest, knowing nobody nor nothing about the damn place. Catch me a nice myocardial infarction. Or malaria."

"Maybe you're scared of the responsibility."

"Diana, with your cash, you could charter some young, hard-muscled professionals with experience to do this. Call your lawyer to hire them. Some clever lads who can buy guns in Guadalcanal or smuggle them in. Bribe the kidnappers or the cops. Third-world place like Guadalcanal, they might be the same jokers. That's the way to get your Rua back."

"OUR Rua."

"As you say."

"You've got experience, Max."

"Less than two disorganized years foundering around, lost in the NYPD. Looking for a soft spot to hide. Academy did not teach us killer karate moves. Nor any Dim Mak Poison Hand fighting techniques. They spent days training us how to call in sick. Me, I'm suspended, discipline-transferred, For-the-Good-of-the-Service. What they call 'a Goofus'. The only reason that I took the job was for the health benefits and the pension."

"Max, we're going to discuss this for just five minutes more. And, then, no more. You'll get back on the plane, flying back to your settled routine life in New York. Won't have to worry about your daughter anymore. I'll handle it."

Diana had won prizes as a debater. I was losing. She was also a rock climber in college and she still kept the same trim look, with catlike strength. Her auburn hair was cut very short, making her look younger. Her face bones and rare blue eyes over tanned cheeks kept the cat look of her. The face worked now, thinning her exquisite mouth. Her eyes turned their full force on me. They called up memories. Something wrapped around me, and I had no idea what to call it. It felt strong.

"Did Walter know that Rua was not his child?" I asked. "Silly question, I guess."

"You're right. Fricking silly. I don't know if he knew. We didn't talk much. It wasn't the world's greatest marriage."

"Not my business," I said. "I'm just stalling."

Another deep breath bought me six more seconds.

"Looking at your body is too risky," I croaked. "It's melting me down to a grease spot. How DO you stay so lovely, after these years?"

"Max —"

"Okay, I'll do it," I said.

"There's no third choice, as you know. But, first, I'll need some things."

We talked and slept into the evening.

"Please loan me a couple T-shirts that you hate," I asked Diana.

Taking them outside, I wrapped the T-shirts around my mitts and went to a thick pine tree. Using palm-heel, bottom fist, side chop, forearm and low kicks, and gliding with footwork, I walloped the tree. I kept it up. After some time, Diana came out to watch.

"You've done two hours workout," Diana said. Living Southern had given her a drawl. "How can someone your age, your size, exercise so much?"

"I want Rua back," I said.

Someone rang the mansion front door bell.

We dressed and opened the door downstairs.

An Asian woman, wearing a US Army olive-drab raincoat, her hair frosted orange on one side, came inside. She carried a tan duffle bag. She unzipped the bag.

"Like, someone is, like, flying to Guadalcanal soon and needs protection," the woman said. "Like, let me show you or absolutely top-of-the-line products here."

Her speech was sprightly. She was doing what speech experts called 'up-talking,' like a Valley Girl.

"Benelli M4 Super 90 shotgun," she said. "Like, world's best shotgun Fires eight shells semiautomatic. Barrel, sawn down to fourteen inches. Overall length is, like, twenty-two inches. Collapsible stock. Weight just six pounds. You can carry it on a shoulder sling."

"I bet," I said. "Who would make such a horrible thing?"

"Designed for police," she said.

"I'll let that one pass," I muttered.

"Sig-Sauer 220 in .45 ACP for a handgun," she said. "Like, knockdown power in a compact package. Smooth, like, operating power, and, like, easy to conceal."

"Do all gun-runners over-use the word 'like'?" I asked.

Diana glared.

"Probably the wrong time to say that I hate guns," I said. "I'm like, irrelevant."

Both stared.

"Always saying the wrong thing," I said. "Mysterious lady, where do you GET these ugly things?"

"My church group sells them to put in a new air-conditioning system," Orange Hair replied.

"Max, stop your damn questions and try growing up," Diana said.

CHAPTER THREE

Blending In
or
Falling My Way

Feeling scared, I caught the next flight to Guadalcanal.

To help Rua, I should try to blend in with the crowd on Guadalcanal.

"Landing at Henderson Field," the man next to me said in an Australian accent.

"New name is Honiara International Airport. But old heads like me still call it Henderson Field. Named for one of you Yank war pilots butchered, fighting the bloody Japs."

"Lot of fighting here," I said.

BLEND IN, I told myself.

"Cor, don't you Yanks know?"

He squinted at me. Nut-brown, grizzled, with some missing teeth, past 80, he looked like a survivor of something horrible.

"Battle here, Guadalcanal, decided the fate of all Asia. On this spot."

"How?"

"Killer Japan wanted it all, Asia. And they actually had it, from your Alaskan islands, to the ruddy gates of India. If they got through

India, the blighters could link up with Hitler's troops in Iran. That happens, nothing could stop those Germany and Japan from taking the world."

"You must be a history reader," I said. "But what does Guadalcanal have to do with all that?"

He grimaced his carved outdoor face.

"Ask around," he said.

"See how long it takes for someone to tell you."

He sank back into his seat.

To keep blending in, I needed him to keep talking with me. Police are such joiners, such football-team types, that they mistrust loners. They pay more attention to those traveling alone. That kind of attention I did not need.

"Why don't you please tell me?" I asked. "It's about time that I learned about it."

"Too right. Trouble with you Yanks, don't know enough about what matters. Happened at Guadalcanal eighty years ago, changed all of Asia today."

"Look at all that jungle under us," I said.

"Hope our pilot's good at his job."

My guide stayed quiet. He seemed to have slipped into sleep. His head tilted. His mouth with missing teeth gaped.

"Clear conscience," I muttered. "Bet he doesn't have a kidnapped daughter on a jungle island, ten thousand miles from home."

Our jet shimmied a bit coming to the landing strip below us. Then we lit rough. My head bounced back on my neck.

"Pilot skill," I grunted.

"Something that you take for granted in the modern west."

My historian seatmate was still in the Land of Nod. His mouth hung open and he seemed at peace.

"Right this way, sir," the Black stewardess in the doorway said.

"And thank you for flying Air Pacific."

"Yeah," I said. "My first trip here."

I tripped.

My left leg caught something on the staircase.

My balance went.

The steps hit me on my way down.

They hurt.

The face of stewardess yawned above me.

She looked way different now.

The hot blue Pacific sky spun above me.

My arms flopped out and back in, and I tried tucking my head and curling into a ball and stopping as the asphalt hit my palms.

"Welcome to Guadalcanal," I panted.

Talking hurt.

A clutch of Black men in light blue uniform shirts above darker pants shambled towards my disgrace.

"Blending in just great," I said. "And here come the local fuzz."

The cops wore checkered baseball hats. The hats made them look like cab drivers. Their belts held batons and tear gas spray holders but no guns.

"How you feel, sir?" one shouted at me, over a sloping big belly and under snow-white hair. He had a sing-song kind of British accent.

"Like I just slid down on a giant banana peel," I said. "Blending in like a champ, that's me."

"Why you fall down, sir?" the white haired cop asked.

"It's a gift," I said.

"You hurt?"

"Left knee, left ankle and everywhere else. Feels like blood on my head. Dizzy. Like I'm gonna pass out."

Fear made me speak faster.

"If I go out, check my heart. You know CPR?"

"What's that? No, sir. We got the air ambulance to Port Moresby, you need that, sir."

"Want to dump an injury to some other jurisdiction," I said. "Typical cop. Get me a paramedic here to check me."

"A what?"

"Ambulance man."

The cop turned and spoke to his pals in a language that was new to me.

One trotted to the airport building, tan, sandy colored and trimmed with green.

The crowd stared at me.

I felt stupid, clumsy and alone, the only White guy in sight.

"What language's that?" I asked.

"That Pidgin."

"Pidgin?" I went on.

"Man, you know nothing 'bout us?"

"Why you in Guadalcanal?" the first cop asked.

"Oh, you know."

"No. Nobody come here. We the worst place in the world, malaria. Come when they got to. Aussies, New Zealand types, no Americans. You American, yes?"

Our foreign policy flashed before my eyes.

"Guilty," I said.

"Then, why you come here? You sell the drugs? You CIA? Why? Gotta tell us why or we put you back on plane straight away!"

CHAPTER FOUR

Dancing Through Lies
or
Mambo This, Copper

He kept shouting.

The other cops moved in.

They clenched around me.

"Prime Minister don't want you coming here anyway!" Snow White hollered at me. Veins corded his neck.

"Me, personally? I'm honored."

"None of you *Jumbles*, no."

"I'm paying airfare and hotel and restaurant money by coming here," I said. "Looking around, I think that you could use the cash."

"Not from you!"

"This is wasting my injury-time," I said. "Such talk honors the unworthy. Never saw a cop like you in my life, discouraging tourism. Do I get an ambulance or not?"

"Why you here?" another cop demanded. He wore gold wire-rim glasses and something red and wet staining his mouth. It looked like he was chewing a tomato without using his hands.

"In New York, I'm a dance teacher," I said. Time for the truth.

"You? Can't be!"

"Wounded am I. How can you tell by looking?" I asked. "What does a dance teacher look like, anyway? Yes, I am. Been teaching dance since Lazarus woke up from his nap."

"Why you come here, man?"

"To open up a dance school," I said. Lying again. It sounded smooth. Maybe I should go into politics. "Would seem obvious. Did you think that I would seek work as a male model?"

"Not with that belly," Snow White said.

"Leave my belly out of this. We grew up together. And now it's hurting. Along with everything else in my body. Where's the ambulance guy?"

"Ambulance very dear and your health insurance don't gonna work here," the one with the wet red mouth said. "Bad stuff for you, mon."

"Look who's talking," I said.

"What is that mess you're chewing? Looks like you're eating your own tongue and spitting it out."

"Constable," Snow White said to him. "Gave you Verbal Admonishment", he made the words into capital letters by the way he rolled them. "About chewing while in The Uniform. Perhaps your name should be sent up."

"Same old cop system everywhere," I said. "Sending your name up. Sounds old-fashioned. But the dance stays the same. What ARE you chewing?"

"Betel nut," the Red Mouth said.

"Charming. You called me '*a Jumble.*' What's that."

"John Bull. Who we call '*Jumble.*' The English White man. Who oppress us Black peoples."

"Race prejudice rears its ugly head anew," I said. "The old reliable. Now, who is this Prime Minister who doesn't want me here?"

"Honorable Bartholomew Doto. We just elect him. Gonna cut our taxes and stop foreign companies from robbing us."

"No more politics," Snow White said. "Ambulance man here."

Two large Black men exited their silver ambulance marked "Good Samaritan Hospital-Guadalcanal Unit" and checked me. They touched my left knee, making me squeal in pain.

They fussed over my whole body.

"This is taking a while," I said. "You fellas aren't too efficient, are ya?"

"No walking on this left knee for a week," the older paramedic said. He was a Black grandfather-type with a four-inch scar pulling his lower lip down.

"At least a week," his partner said. The partner sported bright curly blond hair over his seamed Black face. Maybe he had colored his own hair for effect. Maybe he was a punk rocker in his off hours.

"Sorry," I said. "No can do."

They did not like that a bit. Maybe wisecracking to these two undertaker types ruptured some Guadalcanal taboo.

"You walk on it this week, you may limp for the rest of your time on Earth," the blond Black guy said.

"Now, don't be a crepe-hanger," I said. "All gloomy and such. Maybe I should hear this from a doctor."

The blond man gave me a folded business card with a Dr. Samuel Elutra's name on it

"Doc Sam tell you same thing, mon," he said. His left arm held a tattoo of Bob Marley, the Jamaican singer. Today, it felt like we were a long way from Jamaica.

"Please check my passport," I asked Snow White. "Places want me to get to them."

"Got the Immigration man here," he said. He took my passport from me and showed it to a dried-up man in a crumpled tan uniform who was in my spectator crowd. About ten locals in light-weight tropical clothes clustered near me. Maybe I was local interest.

"Please get me my bag and a cab to the Honiara Yacht Club," I said. "After 19 hours in the air, it's time to rest."

They watched me limp into the cab.

A smallish rust-colored Fiat stayed behind us, in the left lane far back. My driver carried me to a square white building overlooking the Pacific, and I had to lean on the skinny bellman to get inside.

The Black desk clerk shook his fat cheeks under shrewd eyes as he saw me, leaning against the rummy bellman.

"I'm a desperate and dangerous man," I said. "Gimme a bad room."

CHAPTER FIVE

I Ignore My Doc
or
Crippled?

My limbs crackled as I tried lying down on my hotel bed.

Everything still ached.

The left knee was swelling larger every ten minutes.

"Yeah, right," I told myself. "Jungle fighter. That mess we flew over tonight, couldn't see jack. Watch it kill me."

Sometime that night, mosquitoes buzzed near me.

I tried ignoring them.

Good luck.

"I'm snubbing you," I hissed. "In true Park Avenue style."

More buzzed near me.

The thin green mosquito net draped over my bed. Somewhere there must be a hole in the net.

For a while, I slept.

Something stung me.

I rolled.

Something else pricked me, on the bottom.

"Dignity, always dignity," I said.

After another attack, I pulled my US Air Force parka with the fur-lined hood, from the Manhattan Cancer-Society Thrift Shop over my body. When Jymmy had yanked me onto the seaplane, I had been wearing this and was not ready to leave it with him.

This crusade could fall down tomorrow and I would be back in Manhattan's January without my best coat.

Sometime after sunrise, I dressed and limped downstairs to the front desk, ignored the breakfast and spoke to the clerk behind a chipped wooden desk.

He directed me to Dr. Sam, two blocks away on Avenue De La Medana. Blue water waved a hundred yards to my right. This was the fabled Pacific Ocean but I was paying more attention to my knee and all the other body tragedies. The night's sleep had not helped much. The mosquitoes had seen to that.

Locals walked past me, some barefoot and carrying machetes. They looked wiry and worn by hard work.

Already, the sun's heat tightened my shoulder blades.

They stared at me, a *Jumble* waiting outside a doctor's office this early in the morning. After just one night, I was starting to call myself a *Jumble*. Everyone here was Black, except for Our Limping Hero.

The Doctor Sam arrived an hour plus later, a wide and cheery man with thick glasses and a brogue that sounded Scottish.

"You've got a bad knee injury there," he said. "Can't tell more without X-rays. I'll schedule you here at Good Samaritan Hospital. Takes two weeks."

"Give it to me straight, doc. No hearts and flowers," I said.

That was my favorite line with doctors.

"Pardon?"

"How much can I walk on it?"

"As little as possible. Your age and weight are no help."

"Don't help me much, either."

"Without proper rest, heat and physical therapy, your knee could lock up and hamper your walking permanently."

"Doctor, I have to walk."

"Ah, yes, you are probably here on holiday. That is poor timing, I agree. But permanent is quite a long time, isn't that so?"

"D'you have a cane that you can lend me?"

"You should really be on crutches, to heal."

"Crutches would slow me down overmuch. A cane is fine."

"Patients left me several. Here, by the door. Take your pick."

"I need a strong one," I said. "With my weight and age and everything else. This one will do."

"That's a rattan cane, Mr. Royster. Quite a durable and resilient material. Some police use it to give Judicial Corporal Punishment."

"Shoot who?"

"What d'you mean by that?"

"It's a way of asking 'What did you say?'"

"Yes? Very American cowboy. Judicial Corporal Punishment is how some of our neighboring countries dole out punishment."

When in doubt, eat.

The Honiara Yacht Club was just opening up their kitchen when I returned limping. A Black woman, hair tied back with a pink flower and ribbon, bobbed as I entered. Her face split into a professional greeting smile like I was saving her world by dragging myself in here.

Her hair silvered near the temples. She might have been 35 or close to my age. She showed a classic face, with a determined look about her. Muscles bunched under the green smock that she wore. She looked like a strong capable worker, raised outdoors.

A gold tooth glinted on her smile's left side. She seemed like she could leap from smiling to shouting in anger by a split second. Pink rubber thong sandals moved under elegant legs.

"Good morning," I began. "Are you serving breakfast? I could eat that table."

"Yes," she said. She drew out the word the way the locals did here. Her accent was British and precise. "Tea, biscuit with butter and star fruit."

"No. I mean breakfast. Not a snack. Guadalcanal used to be British, right?"

"A protectorate, they taught us."

"Then, let's protect ourselves with some real food. Hot coffee, steak and eggs or corned beef hash. Grits."

"You're not used to our meals, then?"

"That's not a meal. That's punishment. D'you have a menu?"

"For lunch, yes. But usually, we don't serve lunch now."
"Let's make this an unusual day."
Her face clenched.
"Why?" she shouted.

CHAPTER SIX

Finding Food
or
Haberdashery

My nerves screamed.

Something blocked me as I stepped backwards. My ankle barked against it and I fell sideways against the doorway. The rattan cane held me up. My bruises sang sad songs.

"Oh, I'm sorry!" she hollered. She did not sound sorry. "Snarfing down me meds now and them bring bad temper."

Being mad thickened the lilt in her voice.

My eyes hopscotched over her hands. They were empty. The danger had passed.

"You move quick-lee," she said.

"Fear," I said. "Never ending fear."

"You know, we get so little medical stuff here, our systems are not used to them. Like me meds. Because of our diseases."

Her speech changed, from slangy to proper British diction.

"Diseases?"

"Why you are here? Just a tourist. Don't get much of them."

"Disease, please."

"Well, some say that we the world's best place for malaria."

"To catch it or to avoid it?"

"They say to pick it up but I don't believe them."

"Malaria. Diana didn't tell me that."

"Who, Diana?" she asked. "That your wife?"

"Doesn't seem likely now."

"Nobody know much about Guadalcanal. Except war history nuts. They all come here. Looking at our battlegrounds. Even our Ethnic Tension don't keep them away."

"I'm jet-lagged, bruised and starving," I said.

"Too right. For lunch, we got fried chicken, New Zealand lamb sandwich, baked spam, poi or taro."

"Lamb sandwich, please. Well- cooked. And a large coffee."

"Sorry, sir. No coffee. Got tea."

"Tea, then. So long as you don't shout at me again. Where is the nearest clothing store here?"

"Across the street."

"Okay. Is there a drugstore near here?"

"Go out onto Mendana and right about twelve blocks."

"Is there one closer?"

She tossed her head, laughing and smoothed into the kitchen.

Sitting in a shaded corner did not make me think better of Diana.

So I went across the street to a dry goods store and bargained, using just Yankee currency with the aged Asian grandmother behind the counter. My exchange bought three T-shirts, a green jungle bush hat and two pairs of khaki Army shorts with pockets that I kept discovering, light canvas shoes and stout socks, plus a red schoolboy shoulder bag. She let me change clothes in the rear of the store, next to a display for shark repellant. The pictures showed much ripped flesh and blood.

"Please take these winter clothes," I told her. "I'm not schlepping them around in this heat. Keep them in case you ever move to South Saskatchewan."

Feeling right for the heat, I returned to my only personal contact so far in Guadalcanal.

"Here's your tea," she said.

"Why did you laugh at my question about a drugstore that might be closer?"

"Because that such a tourist question! Here, Solomons, we got more than 800 islands, spread out over 11,000 square miles, like the telly tell us. But Guadalcanal got just two damn drugstores. One a block away from the other. Cheek-by-jowl."

"You're joking. TWO?"

"Yessir."

"There must be more. How many people live on these 800 islands?"

"About 600,000, I think. And we are mad iso-lated and suffer from many false backward superstitious fools. Some say the village Big-Man Chief call sharks to their fishing villages, every autumn. Others say, Kakamora tribes hide in the jungle, no contact by outside world. Hidden race of people. Some believe in Kakamora stories, others don't. Old folks say Japanese soldiers still hiding here from the war. See them in the jungle."

"That's impossible. Tell me something, please. At the air-port, some said that they were speaking 'Pidgin English. What is Pidgin English?"

"Don't you know anything? Am I a tour guide?"

"You planning to scream at me again?"

"Not a bit of it. We're mates now, right?"

"Maybe. If you can finagle some coffee."

"That's impossible, I fear. If I can recall what they taught us in mission school, Pidgin English came about cause the traders and the missionaries and such needed to speak to us folks, they invented their own lingo. Solomon Islands got a lot of languages."

"What d'you call a lot of languages?"

"Remember right, we got 70."

"How the devil can a country of 600,000 people have 70 languages?"

"'cause we isolated, I guess."

"More visitors would change that."

"Never happen. Malaria keep them away. No cure for malaria, once they mosquitoes bite you. Guadalcanal the least visited place, the whole world."

"I can't believe that."

"You better. 'tis true."

"This sandwich is wonderful. What's your name?"

"What's YOURS?" she snapped. "Why all these bloody ques-tions? Are you the CIA or something?"

CHAPTER SEVEN

Stakeout
or
What Is Here

"I was right," I said. "You ARE shouting at me."

"Not a bit of it," she said. "But so many questions, Your Grace!"

The proper British schoolgirl speech replaced the slangy island talk again. I wondered what medicine she was taking and why.

"A gentleman should first offer his name to the lady. Then, maybe, if she seems to care, he should ask her name. No further questions. Unless he sees her as just a bit of crumpet."

"Did you say 'bit of crumpet?'" I asked.

"Yes. That's slang here. What you Yanks call some woman for a 'quickie'. Or you call it some 'short-time dirty-leg.'"

"You're an education. How d'you know that I'm American and not Canadian? The accents are the same."

"You're no Canadian. Too fat to be one."

"Wounded am I. You seem to have known a lot of American people."

"Not people. Just sailors."

"We'll let that one pass," I said.

Try to blend in, I kept telling myself.

So far, nothing was working.

The place cheered me up, with bright blue and coral sea murals painted on the butter-colored wooden walls. In the murals, pink mermaids with red or blonde hair, pale skin and jade colored eyes swam from ships and hairy dark sailors. Maybe the barmaid saw herself as one of the mermaids.

Three huge picture windows faced south, next to a side door. My palms curled and flexed, wanting that Benelli shotgun and the Sig-Sauer pistol in them. Guns and I never got along, but I needed them now to get my daughter Rua back alive. Without the guns, Our Hero had no chance.

"Beyond all that, my name is Elie."

"The sandwich was quite tasty, Elie. I'm Max. Do I need this ugly hat to walk around and digest breakfast in your sunlight?"

Part of my plan was to let the Guadalcanal ladies mother me.

"If you don't, you'll fry like an egg. Why were you wearing those heavy clothes before?"

"Came here quickly from a wintry clime. No time to pack."

"We Guadalcanal *pikanini* girls *deem* that suspicious –"

"You keep changing your talk, from schoolish British to Pidgin patois," I said. "Why is that?"

"Haven't spoke to many Yanks in a dog's age. Maybe why."

"I'm honored."

"Leave off on the twenty questions, mate. With the Ethnic Tension shootings about, we are edgy around strangers."

"Can you explain 'Ethnic Tension?'"

"Why? I didn't say a word about it. Not one word. Remember that."

Agreeing with that by bobbing my smiling tourist head, I stepped outside and into the heat.

Guadalcanal's main city, Honiara stretched in front of me.

Houses painted in kid cartoon colors of baby blue and hot pink lined the wide asphalt street.

Green jungle plants sprouted from sidewalk cracks.

A thin stream of jeeps and plantation jitneys bounced past. Slim coconut trees leaned above me. Hairy brown shells lay split open showing whitish meat inside.

A frail-looking man about forty shinnied up a tree. He used a wide blue band around the trunk to raise himself higher. He wore nothing but a pair of khaki shorts.

"The local look," I muttered.

Out in the water, boys swam, whooped and cavorted. Rusted ship hulks pointed skywards. Maybe they were war relicss and I spent some time just watching the Black boys swim near them and thinking how I could find Rua.

"The local look," I muttered, finding a bench under shade.

From jet-lag, I dozed.

Old men did that.

A bit later, I pulled myself awake from sweet sleep.

My Diana memories starting to wrap around me, I tried shaking them free by ambling back to the club. It was getting close to my time to score the guns.

A gambling casino had a rusting ATM that gave me Solomon Island dollars. They bore Queen Elizabeth of England's face, etched in the violet parchment. Outside the casino, somebody's grandmama whacked a broken machete against a coconut shell, cussing in some tongue. As I entered the Yacht Club Cafe, I saw two tables of men in rough clothes munching their lunches. Nobody looked at me. Nobody glanced at me as I sat. That was good, just like I wanted.

Elie smiled like a professional greeter and pushed a cracked plastic menu towards my table.

The Good Gunrunner should be here soon.

Waiting for him felt hard.

CHAPTER EIGHT

Delivery
or
Hard to Ignore

"So, you're back for more," Elie said. "You can't still be hungry. Cup of tea?"

"No, thanks," I said. The tea's caffeine would shake my nerves up. Already, I was jittered about picking up the guns. Carrying guns overseas is illegal, unless you happen to be a US Marine leading an invasion force. So far, Guadalcanal looked like a forgotten backwater. Their jails would be a muddy nightmare, with malaria and short rations.

"Fruit juice?" I asked.

"Best not," she said. "Since you're new here. Body not adjusted and such. And you look a bit delicate."

"But, still too fat to be a Canadian," I said. "Canned tomato juice, from someplace distant and healthy?"

"Right-oh."

"Outside is like a furnace. Can I get some ice with it?"

"I *ting-ting* no."

"What?"

"Sorry. I forgot. You not from here. Our words '*ting-ting*' means 'think'."

"That's Pidgin English again, right?" I said.

"Yeah, man. Pidgin. Ice not for you. Cubes come from local water. Not clean."

"Say no more. No ice, just juice."

Minutes ached by. I could feel them strain past.

Traffic thinned outside the cafe. Maybe the Guadalcanal workers were knocking off for lunch. The locals in my cafe were making noise, chowing down some fried fish and chips lunches. They spoke mostly in English, heavy-slurred and accented. It reminded me of the Jamaican accents back on my NYPD foot beat in Brooklyn.

Sometimes I could not understand a word. That was probably more of the Pidgin English. Or it might be another one of those local languages. Finding Rua was impossible if I could not even gab in the language. They threw the name "Ugi" around. The name angered their talk.

"Ugi want kill me cause my family, born Malaita," the oldest one with strings of beads slung under a black beard turning gray. His bare belly pushed out as he spoke. "Him use terror against us. They do night raids, set Malaita people house on fire."

"Report it to Constable," he went on. "Constable say they know about Ugi. Say they gathering information and collecting data. I say, 'Mon, take action. I know people been gathering information and collecting data they whole damn lives'."

The tomato juice tasted tinny in my mouth. Maybe it had been too long in the can.

The cafe door opened.

This might be the Good Gunrunner.

A reedy youngster, looking South Asian, about eighteen, under a shock of heavy black hair and a struggling moustache, came inside the cafe. He held a canvas sack under one arm. If he was trying to be subtle, he failed. His piercing eyes swept around the cafe. Picking me out was easy, as the only White joker there.

He wagged his head at me, making eye contact.

"Yessir?" Elie said to him. "What you like?"

I slid off my chair. This was turning bad. I better play dumb.

He stepped towards me.

The workers broke from their table. One held up a huge hand next to his crewcut head. A plastic wallet opened in the hand.

"CID," he grated in a baritone. "Halt, in the name of the Queen."

"What?" the youngster said.

"CID," he repeated. "Criminal Investigation Division, Royal Solomon Islands Police –"

The youngster bolted.

He got two feet away.

The other men landed on him.

He kicked at one. Big mistake. They knocked him across the cafe. His sack flew through the air and landed at my feet.

The Benelli shotgun slid out of the sack and hit my foot.

CHAPTER NINE

In the Name of the Queen
or
Pressure Policing

The cops, the CID men, stared at me, my cane and the shotgun. "CID," the one with the open wallet said. "Halt –"

"In the name of the Queen," I said. "I know. Consider me halted."

"Stop squirming about!" another one hollered at the youngster. By now, the youngster was sandwiched between three of them and lying on the plank floor. One sank both of his own knees onto the youngster's rib cage.

"Let the youngster breathe," I said. "He's not going anywhere."

"Shaddup, *waytii maan!*" the bruiser with the knee action said.

"Not going anywhere with about 270 pounds of your Guadalcanal fat on top of him," I said. Always the perfect tourist, I.

My cane was dangling in my left hand and I could swing it into his groin, if I needed to strengthen my message. "More important, if he cracks a rib, he might die. How would you demonstrate the positive side of that event?"

"Don't matter," the Kneeler said.

"It might," I said. "Because you don't know who I am. Think about your job, officer."

"Could bust you up, too!"

My eyes locked his.

"Start whenever you like, officer," I said. "But get off him first. Or else, I'll take action."

My chin tucked down and I stepped in, ready. He saw that.

He got up off the youngster.

As often, being scared made me a regular little chatterbox. Seeing that shotgun had affrighted me.

"He carry dem guns for you!" the cop with the wallet said.

"Me? Don't be silly. I wouldn't know what to do with them."

"You come with us!"

"Following a little white rabbit down a hole in the ground? I don't even know who you are. Look like thugs to me."

"Look sharp," the cop with the wallet said. He slapped it down onto the table in front of me.

It was a bi-fold black plastic wallet with a plastic card window. The pale gray card inside had a photo of this character, with a thinner face and trimmed hair. A fat blue crown lay printed above the words "Royal Solomon Islands Police Force, Jonathan J. Dorris." Some printed lines lay underneath it.

It was time to put the adults off balance again.

"Looks like fake ID to me," I said. "Get me a uniform car here."

They did.

When it arrived, they threw me into it. My cane dropped and Dorris snatched it up.

The driver was a huge brute with a busted nose and missing front teeth. He glared at me and shouted in Pidgin.

"You look like someone who works in a garage," I said. "They use you as the jack."

"Stop spouting off so much," Dorris said. His chest muscles swelled under the work clothes. He stood about three inches taller than my six feet and as solid as police pig iron. His brown eyes scurried over me like I was a piece of furniture that he was planning to break up and throw out with the trash.

"I do nothing bad!" the youngster shouted in a high-pitched South Asian accent. It sounded like he was giggling. But he was not, with blood showing red against his chalk-white teeth. "I get cash to bring –"

"Dorris, since we're chatting so pleasantly, I want the American embassy on the phone and a lawyer," I said.

"Fiji."

"Excuse me extremely?"

"We got no Yank stuff here. We independent, fella. Got a British Honorary Consul. Closest American be in Fiji Islands. Nobody here."

"Then, use your head. You had some training in your police academy, right? What is the charge against me?"

"He bringing them guns to you. Guns are illegal."

"'course they are. I was drinking tomato juice. It doesn't matter what he says to you. He'll say anything to get a lighter sentence. How are you going to explain this to your sergeant?"

"I a sergeant."

"Your superior, then."

"Him don't care. Look these guns. Expensive. New. Likely nicked from somewhere. See the saw marks, shotgun barrel? Criminal element. Someone foreign. And rich. Some fella *blong likkim* you."

"You're getting excited, Sergeant Dorris. Talking Pidgin and such."

"You not a gunman, huh? Prove it me."

"Stay frosty, Sergeant. I got no weapons. I'm just reaching for my worn out bachelor wallet."

"You got a weapon, you never get off the island."

"Don't like guns, Sarge. Here, read this paper. May explain me to you."

"This paper, this you?"

"All of me. Just like the song."

"Dis paper say you was a constable in New York. Lost five vacation days for working three hours overtime without your lieutenant's permission. What's overtime?"

"Ask your boss."

"Eh?"

"Tell him I'm threatening to infect Guadalcanal with the concept of police overtime. Like Columbus bringing syphilis to the New World. Guadalcanal policing will never be the same."

"Disrespect!" the driver spat. He punched at my head.

CHAPTER TEN

Who Goes Where?
or
That Depends

The Driver's fist got bigger.

My knees bent as I bobbed under his right hand punch. He missed my head by three inches.

"Throw a sucker right again," I said, "and I'll take you apart."

He obeyed.

I ducked under his punch again. My foot lifted for an ankle kick, and Dorris slammed into me.

"Stop this," he said.

As I fell against the car, all my Henderson Field airport bruises screamed for attention.

A Black woman towing her kids stopped to stare at us. So did a withered joker wearing just blue jean shorts and broken black wing-tip shoes.

Again, my plan to blend in was not working well.

"Now I know why you jokers didn't handcuff me," I panted. "You wanted to play Pin-the- Punch-On-the-Honky."

"You not want dem guns?" Dorris asked. "Then, why you here, *waytii maan?*"

"Don't call me 'White man' in Pidgin," I said. "I'm starting to understand Pidgin. And I'm not White. This is just a pigmentation disorder. This is why I came to Guadalcanal. Watch."

While they watched, along with the youngster, I pirouetted into a complex American waltz step with a hesitation step and a twinkle at the end. The squad kept watching me.

"I came to Guadalcanal to open up my dance studio," I said, still panting.

They were scaring me. Jail here would be a mess. Rua might get dead or sold as a sex-slave forever. That would break me.

"HERE?" Dorris asked.

"Why not?"

"Guadalcanal? We got de *Suahongi* dance. Use it to pray for good crops at the *Manga-e* ceremony. That funny thing you do, gonna help that?"

His tone sharpened. Sweat sponged out of me.

"Ask me in a month. Your wives and girlfriends will be nagging you to ferry them to my class."

"You don't know nothing about us."

"Or nothing else," the Driver said.

"Where you gonna open, this place?" Dorris asked.

Maybe my hustle was working.

"Just like too many cops everywhere," I said. "You criticize anything unrealistic. You're doing it now."

This was no time to hesitate.

Instead, I spun on my heel, glimpsed a tin Quonset hut across the road and pointed.

"Right there," I said. "Like Babe Ruth pointing where he would plant his next home run."

The Driver started across the road. That scared me. Maybe he would check with the hut's owner.

"Whither are we drifting?" I asked.

"What you say?"

"Where you go?" I asked. This Guadalcanal talk was affecting me, too.

"Talk to this Ruth fella, see if him know you."

"Knock off the Tarzan-talk," I said. "If you see Babe Ruth over there, you better not try to speak to him."

"Is my duty. Why not?"

"'cause he graveyard dead. Lookit my hut. Broom it out in front, fix that broken window, check for snakes and spiders, and it'll look like Lady Gaga's summer home."

"You teach Guadalcanal blokes to dance with stranger women?"

"Why not? What d'you suggest? Sharks are too slippery to hold."

"You crazy," Dorris said.

"Can't be no gangster, though. Too touched, the head. Less us bring this other fool. Leave this mad dancing fool to him own devices."

"Boss be happy we got these guns," the Driver said. "And this idiot."

Maybe he meant me. My insides iced up again. He poked a dirty thumb at the youngster.

"Dis fella here," he said.

Dorris lumbered into the car. It moved down under his weight and rocketed away. The other cops glared at me.

"You the one we should arrest," the younger one said. "We keep watch you, yeah. Make another mistake, we put you in jail where they rape White man in shower every day."

CHAPTER ELEVEN

Rough Stuff
or
Police Brutality

After the Forces of Right left my bruised self and my cane alone in the road, I hobbled across the road to the Quonset hut.

Some locals kept watching me, reminding me that I was not blending in worth a damn.

The tin Quonset door felt hard against my knuckles.

"Come in!" a man shouted from inside.

The door creaked open outwards.

A hand grabbed my arm. I spun under it.

The Grabber was pulling me into the hut. He looked as big as the National Debt. Biceps swelled against me.

As hard as possible, I kicked his right shin and then his left, with the same foot.

"Tap, tap!" I shouted. "Kick-ball-change dance step in the concrete ballet!"

"Raugh!" he said. He hopped backwards, a big wrestler-type in his twenties.

"I hope that's the Pidgin word for 'welcome'," I said. "I'd hate to think of you saying a dirty word to me."

He swiped a hairy hand at me so I shin-kicked him once again.
He toppled to the floor.

"Pardon me," I said. "Guadalcanal police brutality and such.
Perhaps I am a bit overwrought."

"Kicking dirty," he said. "You dirty."

"Aw, your mother moves pianos. Stay down, pal, or I'll fight
really filthy. Being old and fat, I can't fight fair."

Another man, aged, lean, with bluish flowery tattoos curling
up from his shirt collar and down his arms, sat in a beach chair
nearby. He wore sunglasses and a smile that said nothing.

"Was it you, told me 'come on in'?" I asked him.

He was one of these talkers who hummed his words before
speaking them.

"Mmmmmm, preee-cisely," he said. He strummed his own
voice like it was a fine guitar.

"How many cars can you fit into this hut?" I asked.

"Why?"

"Because if Big Fella over here tries for me again, I'm gonna
turn this place into a parking garage."

"Pardon?"

"Pardon nothing. Didn't you ask me inside here? That makes
me your guest. Is that how you treat your guests?"

"Preee-cisely."

"I want to give you some money. Make you rich. And you treat
me this way."

"What's dat?"

"Cash. Lucre. Swag. Pictures of the dead Presidents."

"*Waytii mann*, why you wanna *garem*?"

"What does '*garem*' mean, in Pidgin?"

"'*Garem*', it mean everything."

"Like money?"

"Ummm, precisely."

He sang 'precisely' out again.

"It sure does," I said.

"You've got linoleum floors, not wooden ones, so I'll give you
five hundred dollars, American, for one month's rent. Starting today.
Cash on the barrel head."

"Whose head?"

"More jungle-juice Tarazan talk. See the money? Yes or no?"

"Why you want dis place, *blong* me?"

"Dancing lessons. I'm the teacher."

"You never."

"Goodbye, sir. I'll give this money to one of your neighbors. They'll rent me a place."

"Wait, wait. First, talk with my brother, he own –"

"No good. I came to Guadalcanal, get away from bureaucracy, chain-of-command, all that mess. Take my money now or forget it."

"I take. Taking it."

"So I see. Good. Give me the keys."

"You not polite," the kicked man said.

"Too old for that, too," I said. "Keys."

"Here. Take them."

"Thanks. I'll be in and out of here the next month. See this cane?"

For effect, I whacked the cane against the Quonset tin wall. It TWANGED! like a banjo.

"Anyone comes inside here without permission, I will figure that they're trying to rob or kill me. So I'll slam them first. With this. D'you understand?"

"Us *wantoks* don't do no robs," the joker on my new dance floor said. "Don't know us, *waytii mannn.*"

"I'm learning. Sir. Ex-tenant, is there running water here? Bathroom?"

"Gas station, down street a bit."

"How romantic."

"Want some mosquito nets over those windows, too," I said.

"Why for?"

"Malaria."

He snorted and blew his nose info his fingers. With a thumb, he motioned the other charmer on the floor and both left together.

Tired out, I surveyed all that I owned, turned off the overhead light. "No more work," I said. "Shop closed. Boss he go home. "

I decided to reward myself with a nap on the ground.

"Again, again, I say to you," I whispered. "When in doubt, nap."

My airport bruises agreed with me. The eyes shuttered inside my new hut.

Something woke me.

I squinted near the noise.

A black and yellow snake came at me.

CHAPTER TWELVE

My New Pal
or
Maybe Harmless

The snake kept coming.

"Waugh!" I hollered, still moving. My cane was gone. I couldn't find it. I flung out my right arm and smacked the floor.

Sunlight from the window lit the snake. Yellow mixed with black snakeskin.

He moved to darkness.

I could not see him.

Flipping over, my knees hit the wall and hurt.

Pain made me grip both knees.

But Mister Snake was still somewhere around.

Two windows lay near the door.

I rolled to my feet, sprang to the door, yanked it open and tore outside.

Across the street, the same gentleman with my money in his pocket sat on a rock, watching me.

"Hey, you!" I shouted.

"Excuse me?"

"Sorry. Snake attacks corrode my manners. What's your name?"

"Wyne. Name is Wyne, sir."

"I'll drink to that. You forgot to tell me about the snakes here."

"Ummm, preee-cisely."

"Talk it up, Wyne."

"Oh, mean Rutherford?"

"Guess I damn sure do."

"Rutherford *blong* no problem. Him just move around."

"You bet your life."

"I *ting-ting* him not perilous. What I THINK. *Hokay?*"

"Did he ever bite anyone?"

"Rutherford? Everyone *tok-tok* something –"

"Everyone who talk-talks, they ever just pop off after Rutherford bit them?"

"You worry 'bout Rutherford?"

He made it sound illogical.

"Well, he's definitely going to derail the mambo lesson that I'm trying to give."

"Nobody care."

"For a start, I'll start caring."

To begin that caring program, I peered inside the two windows near the door but Rutherford was not on display.

With a foot, I pushed the door open.

"Rutherford," I crooned. "Wherefore art thou?"

Nothing stirred that I could see.

I switched on the lights and walked the length of the hut. Holes sprouted in the tin walls, easy enough for Old Rutherford to either take his leave or stage a dramatic return.

I went back outside, crossed the street and entered the Honiara Yacht Club cafe. Elie looked at me like I was the Second Murderer from Macbeth but I begged a cardboard box and a blue Magic Marker pen from her.

From my hotel room, I unplugged the portable radio and took it with me.

Back in my Quonset hut, I ripped the cardboard box into four parts. On each part, about a foot long, I used the Magic Marker to write: FREE NEW YORK DANCE LESSONS GIVEN INSIDE.

"That should draw the locals," I muttered.

My watch read two-ten, Guadalcanal time.

"It might be a challenge finding cocktail lounge dance music on the local radio," I rattled on. "But Our Hero must try."

The radio squealed as I twisted the channels.

On the radio, a man's deep voice shouted in a language that I had never heard before. He kept going, mad about something. No soft dance music there.

Another station said, "Welcome to Pidgin radio hour."

Another explosion of words followed.

Another station put out some kind of sugary muzak.

"This is the one," I said. "For right now. All I need now are customers."

Nobody came.

Five chairs were inside my hut so I dragged one outside and tried to look like a successful Manhattan ballroom trainer to the stars.

Nobody gave me a second look.

Time slithered past like Rutherford.

"What you need, son, is advertising," I said.

My knee and other bruises sang painful ditties as I trudged back to the cafe.

"Feel like a schoolkid bringing an 'F' report card to his mommy," I told Elie.

"White men confuse me," she said.

"That's because we White men are only for entertainment. Not to be taken seriously. Some more writing materials, please?"

"You writing books?"

"There's no money in it. Thank you."

"Old Bill hurt you?"

"Who is Old Bill?"

"Thass we call our police. Slang from England. We pick it up."

"England?"

"Yass. We proper English. Queen Elizabeth our boss, too. Celebrate Boxing Day. Play cricket. Drink tea."

"May I put these ads over here by your door?"

"Nobody gonna dance, your place there. Guadalcanal people not like you *ting-ting* we are."

"We'll see. Dancing brings universal love."

"Some husband chase you through the bush with machete, man, *tok-tok* you 'bout universal love."

"How melancholy. What is your favorite dance? Waltz? Rhumba?"

"My island dance. From Malaita. *Tue-tue* dances. Do that, we copy fish and birds moving."

"Sounds mad hot. Anything else?"

"That my only dance, *waytii mann.*"

"Even back in Flatbush, nobody calls me 'White man' so much. It's no honor, believe me."

Outside, I took a cab and directed it to go left, to the east. Stopping at a dry goods store, I caned inside. An Asian man looked up.

"Need a big knife," I said. "Right away."

CHAPTER THIRTEEN

When the Going Gets Tough
or
The Tough Go Shopping

"You ask for knife?" the Asian man behind the counter asked.

"Sure thing," I said. "Just look at this store of yours! I see kids' toys, carpentry tools, tire repair kits, clothes, shoes, sun-hats and canned food. All I need is an outdoor knife for camp chores. Where d'you have them?"

"We don't."

"Excuse me extremely?"

"Ethnic Tensions here," he said in a Chinese intonation that made his tones rise and fall.

"So we cannot sell any pocketknife or flick-knife or hunt knife. Police take my shop away."

"How d'you cut up din-din?"

"Excuse me?"

"Kitchen knives for cutting food."

"We sell machete."

"A machete ruins the tone for a cheery family dinner, huh? Daddy planning to carve up the family roast. Not quite the Norman

Rockwell family image. Norman never saw Guadalcanal. What is this Ethnic Tension you're blowing about?"

"Don't know?"

"Don't know much and that's a fact, Jack."

"Who is Jack? This is Guadalcanal. The next big island is Malaita. Is more old-fashioned than Guadalcanal."

"Hard to imagine."

"Some Guadalcanal people not want Malaita people here. Say they stupid. Dirty. Hurt everything. You have same problem, your country?"

"Sure. Except some call them Democrats."

"We got them shoot at police here. Police, no guns. Got Aussie commandos with rifles, fight back. Ambush police cars, somebody. Laws say, no can sell guns, spears, knives except machetes."

"Only machetes, right?"

"Or police close me down. No knives."

"This bears careful thought. Lemme cogitate. D'you have any good strong canes? This one that I'm dragging around here, doesn't reassure me much."

"Canes?"

"Show me your oldest, most traditional canes, please."

"Don't know, we got canes."

"You got 'em," I said. I hoped so. Now, I was unsure.

"Got no cane," he said.

"You got everything here. Gotta have canes. Look what I'm walking on, this cane. Need a stronger one."

"Look okay."

"I can tell that you're shucking and jiving. Your lips are moving."

I was the one lying because I needed a cane that could kill. But I could not tell him that.

"Excuse me?"

"Canes, *Ah-Sook*," I said.

Those words meant "Older Uncle" in Cantonese. His mouth opened. Maybe he was trying to smile.

He led me to the rear of the store and pointed to a heap of umbrellas and walking sticks. Ignoring my aches, I dug into the pile and tested each cane top. My hands twisted the tops and tapped them.

Something useful might be here. One cane had a white-silver tiger's head on it with a band of fake rhinestones around the neck. When I twisted the tiger's head, it came out, holding a long triangular metal blade.

"Sword cane," I muttered. "Fashionable weapon of a bygone era."

This triangular blade would pierce any material, even a bullet-proof vest, in case Guadalcanal baddies went high-tech. It was going to be my new friend.

Shielding the cane from the Asian man, I weighed it in my hands and tapped the floor.

"Absolutely capital, *Ah-Sook*," I said. "I just fell in love with this tiger."

"Very old, sir."

"Am I that young myself? How much?"

Maybe he knew about the hidden sword inside the cane. Sword canes had started in China, long ago.

"Special price –"

"Skip the oil," I said.

"– of 700 Solomon Island Dollar, this special."

"That's about $115 American," I said.

"Good price."

"You have heat stroke," I said. "But I will call you an ambulance."

"Pardon?"

"Hold it. This Guadalcanal, maybe you're better off if I don't call you an ambulance."

"Ah, you man of good bones. Sent down from Old Man God. Show you something great right here. Something you never see before."

CHAPTER FOURTEEN

And Now For Something
Completely Different
or
Tommy

"You're gonna show me something, never saw before?" I asked the Asian merchant. "Do I need to whistle up my Mommy to protect me?"

"Look," he said. "Tommy gun."

Shocked, I stepped back. He picked up a Thompson submachine gun with a wood stock and grips that shone like good furniture. The barrel was wicked blued steel. A fat drum magazine fitted into the gun.

"Fifty shots of .45 caliber," I said. "What Al Capone called 'the Chicago organ grinder'. Gangsters and G-men, it changed their lives. Ended some of them, too."

"Like this gun?"

"Never saw one of these in real life. Just the movies. Doesn't just strike someone. It mows them down. Nobody survives direct hits, center mass, this one. The US stopped using them after Vietnam. FBI called them obsolete in '72 and switched to the M-16, just like the Army did."

"You want buy it?"

"It may be obsolete but it still works. Kinda like me."

"Seven hundred dollars, American. You American, right? Is good price?"

"You got bullets for it?"

"Fifty here. Three more boxes, same-same."

"I'm looking for Rua, not defending the Alamo."

"Seven hundred, sir. No find a better one."

"Where did you get it? Civilians can't buy them, especially in the South Pacific. Has this Tommy gun been rusting away here since 1945? With your family holding it as a war relic?"

"Is good!" He wheeled around, put it to his hip, aimed it at the ceiling and triggered it.

BOP! BOP! BOP!

The Tommy jumped in his hands. He was pointing it at the thatched ceiling. Some thatch fell onto us.

"Sir, you really want to make a sale," I said.

Smoke rimmed the bullet holes in the ceiling.

"Could set Guadalcanal afire that way," I said. "I'll buy just this lovely cane with the metal top. Your Thompson is a bit too rich for my blood. Or you might feed me to the cops, so you can keep running whatever hustles keep you solvent."

Holding both canes, I left the store and walked past other wooden houses painted in cheerful cartoon colors. Asians filled the street. There were no Black Melanesians here. Bright scarlet-and-gold decorations hung in the storefronts.

Guadalcanal had its own Chinatown. The sword cane looked elegant and innocent in my hand. Some creative cops, like Frank Serpico, used to carry them.

Even heading a two-cane household like now, I looked at my empty Quonset hut dance hall.

"Don't folks in Guadalcanal want to dance?" I asked out loud.

The afternoon creaked past. Rua had been staying at my Guadalcanal Yacht Club Hotel.

That was why I had chosen to stay there, to get close and become accepted.

Twenty years ago, I would be farming the hotel bar for gossip and leads about Rua. But, now dance had wrapped itself around me. Working cases, I always went with my gut. Moving naturally usually paid off.

Maybe now, my luck was running out. Perhaps nobody was going to enter my dance hut here, with Muzak playing on my stolen hotel radio. It could be that I was wasting time when Rua was lying injured somewhere in the jungle.

My gamble might kill her.

CHAPTER FIFTEEN

Ugi Arrives
or
Street Politics

Guadalcanal's first Quonset hut for dance looked lonely as Our Hero put up signs outside. The heat slowed me. It was like sparring inside a sauna.

"You come from Malaita, teach us dance here?" a man asked.

"Come from Bethesda Fountain, Central Park," I said.

No dance students coming made me surly. Maybe my scheme was failing. He smiled and his face changed. Now, he looked engaged and fascinated by what I had to say.

"You can *tok-tok* little me?" he asked. "Maybe you too busy?"

"We can *tok-tok*."

"Everything bad, corrupting us, all come only from Malaita," he said.

"You ever hear about Vegas?"

"It's not *kastom*," he said.

The man's face caught my attention. He had a well-shaped largish head, with quick darting eyes flashing against the very black skin. He might be an actor or a pro track star. There was that aura of attracting attention from him. You were supposed to cheer. His long legs pranced, like he wanted to break into a run.

"Malaita people have money and the new culture," he said. "They permit dancing with strangers' bodies, holding hands. You are not from here, but I think that Malaita sent you to corrupt us."

"Think what you like," I said. "But I decide whom to corrupt. Nobody else does. Why you speaking clear now, con man?"

"Because Malaitans are modern, know computers, they can control us," he said. "Government, police and trade. Hold Marau Island and the famous resort Tupupinamu nearby. Us Guadalcanal people cannot even work there as busboys. I have documents proving that Malaitans want to take over Guadalcanal by illegal immigration here. They forge work permits by the thousands."

"You speak adroitly, good sir," I said. "But you started with broken English to fool me. I'm not here to minister to your delusions. I limped to this backwater to teach dance. Do you wish to learn?"

He spun on his heel and pointed at my landlord, Wyne.

"Wyne, I know you are Malaitan," he said. "That's why you sneak onto our island and hire this stranger to destroy our family value of marriage and children."

That steamed me.

"Now, listen, stupid," I said in my most charming way. "What d'you know about dancers? Or anything else? Dancers have solid marriages and kids, just like real people do."

He was making me shout.

"Can't talk sense with you."

"Your sense ain't the same as my sense," I said.

"And I know you, too, Ugi," Wyne said. He kept smiling, that same smile that meant nothing. "You always like to start trouble to feel important."

The younger man, who I figured by now was Ugi, swaggered away. He went down the roadway to a roofed shelter where some others were hanging out.

"Street politics?" I asked Wyne.

He smiled and shrugged. Noise down the road blossomed. From Patrol, I knew the rhythms.

Sure enough, Ugi flowed back with a knot of loudmouths who looked gainfully unemployed. Some held chunky brown bottles of something called SolBrew, the Guadalcanal answer to Budweiser.

"All you cats need is to get more drunk while you're just hanging out," I said aloud. Everyone ignored me. Just like back home.

"Listen, my brothers," Ugi clamored. "They try to take our island, our Guadalcanal, away from us and make it part of Malaita! We let this?"

"Ugi, that not our problem," one beer-drinker with a huge belly said.

"Are you men?" Ugi asked. "Then, act like men."

"Ugi right," one said.

"Far right," I said.

"Ugi, my family came from Malaita forever *beaucoup* long time," Wyne said.

"And you know it. We no different from you."

"Got this hut. Big house. Two jeeps. We got nothing, work all time. You cheat us to get rich."

"Leave my uncle peaceful!" another character said, coming across the road. He looked about 17, baseball hat slanted over a marijuana leaf T-shirt and blocky muscles in his arms and legs.

"Lemuel, go home," Wyne said.

"Somebody send junior home," Ugi said.

Lemuel leaped at Ugi, punching at him. A bum grabbed Lemuel around the waist. Lemuel struck him. Two more hit Lemuel.

"Stop this!" Wyne shouted. "He my sister boy."

Everyone moved, including me. Wyne hit Ugi in the gut. I slammed one thug's shin with my cane and dropped him. Ugi wrestled Wyne away, ripping his own shirt.

"That's enough, my brothers!" Ugi cried out.

We all stopped.

"We just defend ourselves," Ugi said. He acted like nothing had happened. "No dancing here by this Malaitan thief. Or else, his house catch fire one night."

"Try it," I said, without thinking.

"*Waytii mann* make threats, us," Ugi said. "Like he own us. Like always. Take our land, our *kastom*, our women, leave us nothing. We go away peaceful now. But we come back."

CHAPTER SIXTEEN

We Dance
or
Culture

My Quonset hut door opened.

Elie the barmaid entered. Two women trailed her.

"Come learn to dance," I said.

"I bring my girlfriends –"

"And you should," I went on. "You're going to love dancing like I do, like we all do."

"This Lorna in the green, and this Miss Hester."

Elie wore different shoes now. She had switched from her black waitress shoes and now wore lime-green wraparound thing boots. The green contrasted with her ebony skin.

"Let's open up big and keep it clean," I said. "Like Dean Martin used to say."

"Who is Dean Martin?" Elie asked.

"Never mind. The explanation would take too long."

"Dance?" one of the women, Mrs. Hester, asked, with a pensive look on her face. She moved like my school had hidden Claymore land mines under the dance signs. She looked like a professional woman, maybe a chief clerk somewhere in Guadalcanal's middle class. She stood a few inches shorter than Elie and her body seemed to burst in all directions from inside an orange dress.

"Right away," I said.

On the radio, my muzak died. A loud buzzing roared from the speaker. We all stopped.

"Means bad luck," Lorna, the other woman said.

She wore a dark green dress with red Valentine talking hearts stitched into it. Her hair was teased into a breath-bouffant over a sour disapproving mouth. She looked like she had spent some time dressing and making up tonight

They made noises like people leaving a place. My teeth gritted together.

The radio cleared. A song came through and I recognized it.

"That's 'Pretty Blue Eyes'," I said. "Wow! That was Steve Lawrence's first big hit."

"When that?"

"I can't remember. Maybe 1959."

"What that like, that 1959?" she asked.

"Different."

"You try joking, yeah?" Elie said. "Listen to the words."

Obediently, I listened.

"They changed the words," I said. "The chorus keeps singing 'pretty brown eyes'. Not 'pretty blue eyes'. It's the same song except for that. The original said 'blue eyes'."

"Why they change words?"

"Probably because a song titled 'Pretty Blue Eyes' would not sell well in Guadalcanal. It lacks the local color."

"'cause nobody here got blue eyes?"

"No more sociology," I said. "Let's dance."

She hesitated. I did not. We went into a slow foxtrot.

At least, I did. Elie just hung on.

Her feet seemed to drag.

"D'you like working at the hotel?" I asked her.

"Is okay."

"Men coming in from everywhere, mostly buying drinks, trying to –"

I let the words hang.

"– chat me up?" she suggested.

"If that's the British slang for it," I said. "Trying to tell you stories, like 'Who Hit Annie In the Fanny with a Flounder?'"

"Other jobs, copra factory, canning tuna, not much better."

"Only men in business come to Guadalcanal," I said. "We need some more ballroom dancing here. No women tourist to Guadalcanal, I bet. Not at your hotel."

"One woman came. American. She go away later."

"Older woman, birdwatcher type?"

"No. She young. Like college girl."

"Where did she go, anyway?"

"Nobody know."

"Do you have to register the guests yourself?"

"Sometimes. When my boss, busy somewhere."

"Where did she come from, in America?"

"Dunno."

Tomorrow, I would follow up.

The song ended and I danced two more dances with Lorna and Mrs. Hester.

Then Success arrived. A bent, sunblasted Black man, older than me, came through my door. His hair and short beard showed gray, white and blond tufts but he grasped Mrs. Hester into a rhumba.

He moved like a dancer from the 1940s. Maybe he had been. The song ended.

"Most refreshing," he said, in the local cadence. "Now, we want no violence here, sir. But I have bad news for you."

CHAPTER SEVENTEEN

Patchwork Police
or
Acts Like Me

All four of us dancers looked at the man.

"Teach dancing without a permit against our law," he said.

"Who you, sir?" I asked. "Voice of my conscience or something?"

"Sub-Officer Soaki," he said. "Royal Solomon Islands Police Force. Look."

His hand gnarled around a blue patch. The patch showed a Queen's crown above the letters RSIPF around a cluster of plants.

"Is that a shoulder patch?" I asked. "Never, in the world, did I see any copper identify himself by a shoulder patch. Lookit my police proof."

"What you mean, sir?"

"Here's my police ID. A punishment."

"So old. Letter so dirty, sir. I cannot read it."

"You're not missing a thing. You call yourself a Sub-Officer. By the way, just what is a Sub-Officer?"

"Yaaas," he said, like he was thinking it over.

"Are you still sworn?"

"Why not?"

"You look like, possibly, you might be," I groped for a word, "super-annuated."

"Too old? Nossir. Royal Solomon Islands Police Force got no maximum age limit."

"Maybe I'll join," I said.

"You remember my name?" he asked me.

"It's a distinguished name," I said.

Maybe flattery would help. That phrase was a con-man line from my time in Patrol. Sometimes that phrase worked to open up street people.

"Yessir. My brother was a policeman, too. Rebels shoot him in ambush. So I cannot quit."

"I getcha," I said. "Blood kin. Like Rua. Sub-Officer Soaki, since you're off-duty and I'm a foreign national, ignorant of your laws, can I apply for a dance teacher license tomorrow?"

Looking like a judge, he thought it over.

"Maybe about noon, when we open?" I suggested.

"You trying to fool this old policeman?" he asked. "Because I a little slow, maybe? And Black?"

"No, sir."

"By this time tomorrow, you best have the license," he said.

"I'll get it. Please feel free to stop by and check. And bring some other policemen, just to make that everything is kosher."

"Kosher?"

"Legitimate, I mean. In the meantime, we should dance."

We danced more. A knot of locals clustered in my doorway.

"Nev-ver seen this but in the moving pictures," another patriarch said to his pal, both hovering at the entrance.

"Welcome, gentlemen," I said. "Please come and dance."

"Just like the movies," he said. "Hollywood and Vine."

Elie favored them both with one of her smiles and that hooked them onto the dance floor.

Somehow, more kept coming into my Quonset hut and trying to dance.

Going for delicate, I did not try teaching a class. Let them comfort themselves by doing what they wanted tonight.

A youngster brought his own laptop and played what sounded like local songs. It was no time to ask.

"Can you keep open this away?" Elie asked me.

"Constables pretty dumb bunnies here, like you see."

"Yep."

"Good dancer, you. Got a wife, girlfriend back in America?"

"No, not anymore."

"No? What happen?"

"Still not sure," I said. Somehow, I tried to keep my tone level. "All I know is that it hurts."

"*Co*! Talk about!"

"'Your word '*co*' is more Pidgin?"

Dancing moved into the late night until we had about twelve couples pushing each other around on my floor.

"Dunno. Everyone say '*co*'."

"Let's talk languages," I said. "Not love."

"Why? You still hurt by some gal?"

Dancing made the time spin fast into night. At the right time, I started asking about other Americans here while I danced the foxtrot.

"You the first American here," a large woman wearing a blue 'sarong and suede shoes muttered.

"They afraid of us Melanesians."

"Pardon me but what are these Melanesians you're talking about?"

"That us Black Pacific people. Guadalcanal got Black population. Not many Whites. Malaria fright them off, too. Mosquitoes, right?"

My hopes sagged.

Another couple fox-trotted past us. The music playing was the theme from *Exodus*.

"You wrong, gal," the man said.

"Yank girl was just here last week."

My feet froze.

Did he mean Rua?

CHAPTER EIGHTEEN

Gab
or
Probably Politics

The dancing man tilted his weathered face, tattooed under both eyes, at me and moved his stocky shape closer.

"Nice bit of girl," he said. "And polite. Not like holiday tart-type."

"Where is she now?" I asked, too fast.

Rushing like a rookie could shut things down.

His dance partner shook her head over a large belly wrapped in a tan dress with red piping over the shoulders and hips.

"Don't be talking so much," she said. "Always chatter like a bird. We not supposed, have these ones, Guadalcanal for ourselves."

"Dass what Doto say all the time," the man said.

He muttered something in Pidgin that sounded dirty. The woman's eyes closed and then opened.

"Doto get you, talking about him," she said.

"Militia take steps."

"What militia?" I asked.

"They off-duty constables," she said.

"No, they not. They rabble."

"I don't know local politics," I said. "Just trying to the pay rent teaching ballroom. I love dancing."

"Better you dance away from here," the woman said. "While you able."

"Just trying to duck cold weather," I said. "Traffic jams and the Number Six IRT subway train."

"Ugi get after you," the woman spat. "Take your money, maybe kill you. Him a bandit."

"He a patriot," the man said. "Doto a bandit with his government protecting him. Bodyguards, gangsters, cashiered soldiers. Say he gone protect us. Protect us from what? Who say we need protecting?"

"Dangerous times," she said.

"Don't try sounding dumb," he said. "You graduate same school as me. Both pretty smart. So, why you trust Doto?" He pointed with his chin to a part of the wall. The letters "UGI" were painted in red.

"What's going on here?" I asked.

"People come to Guadalcanal from the island Malaita," the man said. "They work, buy houses. Raise families. Six years ago, troubles start when some Guadalcanal bad ones want Malaita folks to leave and go back home. Malaita folks say no, been here since the Jap war start. Your own Marines bring Malaita men, build that Henderson Field airport while Japs still shooting them. You think Malaita people just give up 75 years of work and family just cause they born on a different island?"

"You such a speaker, Josiah," the woman said. "Maybe, yeah you run for Prime Minister, youself."

By now, the song had stopped and other dancers were listening to this debate.

"This Ugi sounds radical," I said. "In the Middle East, radicals sometimes kidnap tourists for cash. Does Ugi do that here?"

"He do anything!" another woman, frail, in a yellow dress with a plunging back line showing her spine.

"He protect us when boss-man cheats us!" the man said. "Nobody else does."

His dance partner jabbed her chin at me.

"Why we all talk so much front, this *Jumble?*" she screeched. "He could be a spy, get us trouble."

"Ugi got no white man spy," the man said.

"Doto man, more like."

"Thass enough dancing," the woman. "We too scared, stay here anymore."

CHAPTER NINETEEN

More Politics
or
Blow-Up

"My *wantoks*," the man hollered.

"We go home now. But, Mister *Jumble*, we peace-loving Black people!"

They applauded.

They left, some limping from their steps.

"Buy me a drink?" Elie asked. "After dance?"

"Five years ago, yes," I said. "Six drinks. But, this decade, Our Hero is tired."

"You tired?"

"Just a tired old man, sitting by the side of the road. Staring into a bleak old age."

"That means no?"

"Tonight, yep. Maybe tomorrow, I'll feel younger."

"How you do that?"

"Ask me tomorrow. By morning, my body bones'll crackle and clank whenever I pull myself out of the bed, romantic mosquito netting around it."

"Don't need nets. Malaria no problem."

"For thee, but not for me."

Putting myself into the bed felt too good, after hours of dancing. Sleep covered me like a lover's kiss.

When I woke the next day, strong sun was already stroking the mosquito netting.

Creaking to my feet, I saw that my gut had seemed to grow while I had slept.

"Miraculous," I muttered. "Marvel of the ancient world. Dance till you drop and still get fat."

No matter what angle I took, the belly stayed.

"Hello, front desk," I said aloud. "Know we got no phone here, but if we did, I'd say 'Send up a bellhop with a scale, to weigh the White devil on the top floor'."

The White Devil suffered a cold shower and dressed.

Caning my way down the wooden steps to the cafe, I glanced at the hot green jungle plants all around. Dew was drying on leaves.

WHAMM!

Something blew.

Things hit me.

I went down.

A smell of hot wood buzzed my nose.

My eyes shut.

Something sharp might blind me.

I wanted to run.

"Stay down!" I hissed to myself. "Running getcha killed very dead."

Fear pushed me down, rolling blind until something stopped me. It felt like a tree trunk. Mad, I scrabbled around it and lay against the trunk for cover.

"Wazzup?" I sputtered.

Smoke smell covered me. So did a gristly red-meat smell. The memory came back from Patrol. Someone's skin was on fire. Men shouted.

"Get down, you!"

"Get off me island!"

"We *blong* here!"

"Doto militia!"

"Who's who?" I muttered. My eyes opened.

A blue van lay smoking thirty feet from me. A man in a green pastel shirt hung from a van window. Another man lay alongside. Flames torched clothes on his body. His hair smoked.

Pushing myself up, I stooped to get near him. I tried swatting the fire in his hair out. My palm singed. I grabbed his head by the hair and dropped my thigh down on him and smothered the flames.

My thumb went against the big artery in the throat. Nothing pulsed. I tried again. There was nothing to feel.

"Graveyard dead," I rasped. "Always hurts."

Gunfire cracked. Another man waved a long-barreled shotgun and triggered a blast.

"Go back Malaita!" a woman's voice shouted.

A green taxi flashed past. Guns shot from inside. Sunlight caught the brass shells flying out automatic.

"Kids! Get flat!" a woman shouted. "Don't get shot!"

"You're talking to the right man," I said.

Smoke drifted more.

A green Army jeep rocked to a stop in front of the burning van. A White man in khakis pointed a gun at me.

"Steady on there!" he shouted with an accent.

My hands froze.

Smoke clouded everything.

"American!" I shouted. "Frightened bystander!"

"Yeah?"

"Innocent, too."

"No nacking about," he said.

"Don't know what 'nacking' is," I said.

"Awww. Then don't do anything."

"My specialty," I said.

Others crowded near. They wore khakis, slanted broad hats and carried stubby assault rifles. They prodded the dead bodies with their feet and pushed them aside.

"Bombings be something new for this lot," my guy said. "That is, awww, up to now."

"You look and sound like a boss," I said.

"Interesting," he drawled. Through the noise and shouts, his accent sounded Australian now. "How can you tell?"

"The way you hold yourself," I said. "Makes me bristle."

"Awww, why would you get bristly with me, cobber?"

Women shrieked nearby. Some ran into the jungle, holding babies in their arms.

"What the devil is going on?" I asked, trying to get up with my cane.

"Awww. Ethnic Tension. Are you a reporter?"

"Don't know what I am."

"Guadalcanal folks want Malaita natives to leave. Both sides are shooting at each other."

"How can they tell who comes from Malaita?" I asked.

"Awww," he said. That word "awww" was starting to chafe my inner ear. "Don't know how, but they know."

"My ID here, explain everything," I said, reaching to my pocket.

"Don't!" he said.

The gun came up to shoot me.

CHAPTER TWENTY

A Soldier Is Not A Cop
or
Not Even A Rookie

"You damn *drongo!*" the soldier shouted at me.

His gun barrel bobbed at my soft parts.

"I'm not moving," I said. My voice warbled everywhere, climbed high and broke.

"See? Hands right where you can see them."

The gun kept moving.

"You're in charge," I went on. Maybe my Freudian-analyst tone would calm him.

"I'm not doing anything until you tell me to."

He glared at me. Standing at a right angle to me, he seemed too frail to be a soldier, let alone a commando-type. He stood about five feet seven inches and topped the scale at about one hundred and sixty pounds. Blond hair showed under the wide hat, against pinkish skin that would burn without ever tanning. His arms and wrists showed muscles from discipline and constant workouts, not Mommy and Daddy. His grayish eyes narrowed, making me guess that he had seen action and killed men.

"Staff Sergeant Janos," he said. "Australian Army. Don't reach anywhere, in this here. See all these women and ankle- biters here? Need protection, mate."

"I guess, when you say 'ankle-biters,' you mean kids."

"What else? What are you doing here?"

"Why?"

"'cause Yanks don't come to Guadalcanal. Fighting, malaria, nothing to do. Haven't seen an American here in months."

"Can't tell by looking. Could be Canadians, Brits or some other paleface."

"Bollocks," he said. "Less than one percent of Guadalcanal is Caucasian."

"Let's stop arguing demographics at gunpoint," I said. "You want to frisk me, hop to it. I never carry."

"'Frisk'?" he asked.

"Sorry. Yank slang. I mean 'search.' Go ahead and search me."

"Hands on your head. Cross your ankles. Move and I'll kill you."

"Sounds serious."

"Step back. You an agitator?"

"Only in hotel bedrooms."

"You move those civilians back!" my gunman Janos hollered at the men dressed like him and holding their own guns poised. "Keep your eyes on that tree-line! Fingers off the triggers! Challenge before you shoot!"

"Nobody's talking, Sergeant!"

"As usual," he said.

He prodded my ribs with his gun barrel.

"You, what did you see?"

"I don't see much but I am watching a foreign soldier threaten an American citizen illegally with his gun," I said. "For no reason. Because that citizen, who is I, was wounded and knocked flat by a terrorist bomb. What would your lieutenant say about that?"

"Bollocks."

"How you talk, you big island commando. When and if you calm down, and I figure out which side has justice, I'll tell you what I saw. Not before."

"While you're deciding, one of these aborigines may decide to blow YOU up —"

"I'm not taking sides yet, Sarge. I'm here on Guadalcanal to teach dance and live easy. If I like the place."

"You'll like it, all right. You Yanks should be grateful the island existed in the war. Your country owes these locals a lot."

"America owes them a lot?" I said. "What are you talking about?"

"You'll see."

The bombed-out van lay on its side, like a thrown steer. Orange paint letters read 'Ugi Rules!'

"Somebody writes 'Ugi Rules' on the vehicle and some other johnny blows it up. Why?"

"It was written before somebody put the blast on the car," I said. "The paint is already dry. So maybe you soldiers will think that this cat Ugi did it. But what if Ugi's enemies did it? What terrorists call a 'false flag operation'. That's when you put the blame on somebody else."

"That the truth," a Black man nearby said. 'You an American. So you brave, smart."

"You think that all Americans are brave and smart?" I said.

"I've got bad news for YOU."

KA-RUMP!

Everything shook.

CHAPTER TWENTY ONE

Truth-Shooting
or
The Revolution Starts Tonight!

Again, I hit the dirt. More dirt rained down. Clods went inside my shirt collar.

"Damn!" I shouted. "This is too much of a bad thing."

Someone slammed into my ribcage. It was Janos.

"Bloody bleeding Black Abo fool scum-suckers!" he shouted. "Cannibals!"

Shots fired.

Staying flat seemed smart.

I got up.

A youngster ran through the trees far ahead. This runner was the only one inside the jungle, about six feet three inches tall and rangy. Sunlight glinted off glasses on his face and then he was gone. He might have been twenty-years old.

Janos fired from the hip. Then he shouldered the assault rifle and triggered it again. He was shooting where the Runner should be fleeing, into the brush nearby.

Slugs ripped leaves off.

"Hold all fire!" Janos shouted. "None of you blodgers better shoot! Weapons down!"

"Sarge?" one chunky soldier asked.

"No more shooting. Too many civilians gadding near."

"How'd you miss him, Sarge?" someone catcalled from the brush behind us, hidden by trees.

"That's an Aussie accent asking that, Janos," I said. "One of your men. And it's a good question. You had a clear field of fire from where you were. And that burp gun you got, that can sure deliver the mail at close range."

"You know guns, eh?"

"Too flipping much," I said. "Think you're shooting over their heads. Which is fine with me."

"Really?"

"Sure. We need the military, to keep peace. Defend us. When it's really needed. Rest of the time, sing those rousing marching songs, run, keep in shape, spread that Aussie goodwill everywhere, show those beautiful uniforms and fire over their heads. Everyone just shoot to scare, never to kill."

"Yank windbag, you are, for sure. I do my job."

"By not killing that runner. You're right. I agree."

"Who cares what you agree with? Blodger like you. This Abo who ran, what'd he look like?"

"Don't ya know?" I asked. "YOU shot at him."

"Didn't see much. Not to describe, anyway."

His Aussie accent drew out the word, sounding like 'deee-scriiibe.'

Something held me back. The runner had sported eyeglasses. That made him stand out in Guadalcanal, where few wore specs. If I described the runner with eyeglasses to Janos, I would be getting deeper into this war mess while Rua needed me. This was wasting too much time already.

"Didn't see much," I lied.

"No?"

"My eyes, terrible," I said. That was the truth.

"Garn –"

"Jungle humidity, steams up my contacts. Not used to it. Couldn't see much of him."

"You're lying, mate."

"Don't drag me into your jungle bush war. Isn't my fight."

"If you want to live here, it is," a voice said behind me. "Some Guadalcanal bonkers be wanting exterminate everyone against them."

Wyne, the elder statesman from my Quonset hut dance school, shifted his weight while talking to me.

"Wyne, You just come in and out of the jungle like smoke?" I asked. "I'm seeing that a lot. That the Guadalcanal style?"

"Yaaass." Janos snorted.

"The bonkers, the fanatics, wanna kill everyone against them?" I asked Wyne.

"Yeah," he croaked. "Just like when the Japanese fought here."

"Go climb back in your coconut tree, old man," Janos snapped. "We've got soldiering to do here."

"Truly?" Wyne asked.

"Damn right. You, Yank, again. What did the kid look like?"

"Guadalcanal saved the world," Wyne said.

"You're making it up, Wyne," I said. "How?"

"I'm not mucking here for no history lesson," Janos said. "We got dead, wounded here. Yank, if you don't help us with a description, gimme your passport now."

That shook everything inside me. Without a passport, they would deport me and I would never find Rua.

"Go and whistle for it, as you folks say," I managed to say.

"I mean NOW."

"You got the burp guns and the recruit types making fun of you here already," I said. "I know the recruit look. Are you going to play cop, too?"

CHAPTER TWENTY TWO

Aftermath
or
History Lesson

"Last time," Janos said. He leaned into me. The slung gun poked my ribs.

"Don't tell me what you saw, I'll have you Transported With Prejudice," he rasped. "Dya know what that means, cobber?"

"Guess it means deported," I said. "Deported from this malaria mosquito swamp? Must live out my life elsewhere? O Death, where is thy sting'?"

Janos uttered a rascally gerund and peacock-walked away, his burp gun, ammo packs and canteen slung like Christmas tree trimmings.

Pidgin that I had overheard before came back to me now. The phrase for goodbye seemed right for this moment.

"Okay *lookim* you!" I shouted after Janos.

"*Waytii mann blong tok-tok* Pidgin!" a local with a blooded left leg sang out. "Him *blong* rare bird!"

"How you *staap*?" Wyne asked me.

"Got it," I said. "That's Pidgin for 'hello'. Ask Sgt. Janos there, the one walking away mad."

"You vex him?" Wyne asked.

"With bullies, I usually try to."

"Stand back, you lot," an Aussie tan uniform hoisted a dirty grey stretcher over the wounded lying on the ground. An ambulance, in gray and red trim, with the words "St. John's Ambulance Service" stenciled on it, bumped to a stop nearby.

"You've got about a dozen lying dead or hurt," I said. "Need more than one ambulance."

"Guadalcanal got two," Wyne said. He was back to talking broken English now. Maybe the shock did it.

"Two? Just two ambulances? For the whole island?"

"We poor."

"And dying younger than everyone else."

"No matter. You save my life," Wyne said.

"We talking World War Two history again?"

"No, today. Ten minutes past. When the bomb explode, you knock me down, cover me with your body. Rocks, tree parts come down. Hear you shout. Blood squirts, some on my hand here. Your blood. This time, I got my eyes closed. But feel the rocks, stuff hit your body."

Shock rolled me again.

"Wasn't me, Mr. Wyne."

"Yes, 'twas. You call me this, old man, senile?"

"Never."

"Was you."

"Believe me, if I had done all that, I would sure know."

"Was you," he said. "Lookim blood, my hand. Come from you."

"That's a lot of blood there, between your wrist and pinky. But I'm not cut anywhere. So it can't be me."

"Maybe you mouth bleed inside. You never know. Stop bleed now."

"Wasn't me."

"You the only one near, *blong* me."

He surprised me with a hug that wrapped strong arms around my bruises. Somehow, he had stayed fit while getting old.

"Hold on," I said. "Maybe it was the Runner who covered you. That's what I decided to call the youngster that ran away into the bush. The one that our dear Sarge Janos fired at."

"Was you, Max."

"Feels good that you recall the name."

"You save me. Like Americans save Guadalcanal."

"Back up there, Mr. Wyne. I thought that Guadalcanal saved the world."

"First, you save us."

"Whole lot of saving going on."

"We old know this story. Before you US Marines land here Lunga Point, Japanese own the world."

"Not the whole world," I said.

"Our world. Got the islands here, fighting and beating Chinese in China. Singapore, Malaysia, Thailand, Indonesia, no bloody body can stop them. Nanking, they make fathers rape their own daughters or kill whole family. Burn them alive. 300,000 go dead. They at India, they at Alaska, your land there. Got us here. Nobody *blong* anywhere, protect us. Take us, make us slaves, their plan."

"What plan?" I asked.

"Plan build that air strip. You know?"

"Why?"

"Japanese want *takim* Australia."

"Impossible. You can't know this, Wyne, but Australia's just too damn big."

"That why. So big, they can't defend. Japs good infit- infistr –"

"Infiltrate," I said.

"Sneak ashore somewhere unprotected on the Australian coast, murder a village and then land more troops, tanks and artillery. Before the Aussie army could stop them, thousands would spread everywhere."

"They make that air strip, now Henderson Field, they can fly planes Australia, bomb cities, scare *olketa*, all fella, make them surrender like Singapore. *Haem daefinis*. Dead. Murder machine. You Marines see them building air strip here, beat and kill us Black fella, savvy why they want airplanes fly from Guadalcanal. They fella do that, they win Pacific war. Maybe world."

"You're saying that's why our Marines landed here, to take that airfield?" I asked.

Wyne was starting to bore me but my manners, from Saint Blaise's School for Young Men, stopped me from showing. The private school courtesy held, even on Guadalcanal.

"Yaaas. Planes *blong* way to beat everyone, *olketa*, that war. Japs savvy. Marines land, fight Japs, take airstrip. Night, Japs surprise them, kill many, get near airport. If get it, maybe win war."

CHAPTER TWENTY THREE

Dance At Last
or
Have A Blast

"Hold up a second," I said. "You're trying to tell me that winning this war depended on one night battle between the Japanese and our Marines?"

"Yaaas."

"Can't be."

"*Allfella blong* Guadalcanal, my age savvy this. Japs make us slaves, work Japs airstrip. Marines stop them."

"Have to read up on that."

"Just like you save me. I tell *olketa*. Everyone."

"Please don't. I'm just here to make a new life for myself and teach dancing. No civil war stuff."

"Eth-nic Ten-sion. That President Doto word."

"My plan for today is to go back to the Yacht Club, shower all this Ethnic Tension off me and be giving dance lessons by one o'clock. Okay? Stop by, if you want."

Aware that everyone kept watching this fool White man tourist, me, I did just that.

Tongues kept wagging in Pidgin and English about Ugi and the bombing. Some of the Pidgin was clear enough for me to follow but most was too fast. To keep my image going as a rich eccentric, I bought some more flowered local shirts and black slacks in Chinatown. The local dance king must change his wardrobe often. Fred Astaire always did.

Opening up the Quonset hut and scribbling new signs felt like home again. Rutherford the snake made an appearance. But I had been expecting him and stayed calm. He lay along the wall and seemed to watch me

"You teach us dancing?" one hefty woman wearing a pink sarong and balancing a straw basket on her head asked me.

"Sure do," I said. "For free. No charge. Get your husband dancing and holding you close. Remind him why he married you."

She giggled. So did her lady market pals, all holding baskets head-high and stepping into the hut's shade.

"Bride price, that's why," she said, showing missing teeth.

"What is 'bride price'?"

"Don't wanna tell the *waytii mann dat nomoa*."

"We're back to that 'White Man' routine again? Tell me about bride price."

"*Yufella* fine out too late, *nomoa*."

She giggled again and I saw how she used to look in her teenage years.

"No now. Mebbe later youfella savvy," she said.

"Tell me now. I keep getting older every day."

"Mebbe show you later," she gurgled.

Her hair bounced and she laughed with her whole body.

"She crazy mad, always happy," another woman said.

"Even though, she from Malaita and the GRA, Guadalcanal Republican Army, shoot her son in the buttocks."

"Why did the GRA shoot her son?"

"'cause they Malaitans. From that other island. Malaita folk get power here, Guadalcanal. Most police government bosses, Malaita Johnnies, control *olketa*, everything."

"I know that I asked this before, but how can they tell who is from Malaita and who from Guadalcanal?"

"Dem savvy."

"But how?"

"We savvy us."

"They some fella block roads this town Honiara and stop all Malaita Johnnies," another woman holding a large pink water gourd that looked like baked clay. "No travel, no."

"Can't the police –"

"Police bad. Naogud. No gun. Take side, Malaita Johnnies. No help us."

"The cops are from Malaita?" I asked.

"Yass. Most. Like English do, us call police 'Old Bill.' British run us. We copy they."

"Why do the Brits call their cops 'Old Bill'?" I asked.

"'cause English Sir William Pitt start the first police. Call police 'Old Bill' because of Pitt."

Behind me, my hotel radio was playing "Once Upon a Time" by Tony Bennett. Without asking, I took the laughing woman into dance position and moved forward.

"What you do?" she sputtered.

"Dance, Abigail!" one woman shouted. "*Wiff waytii fella, blong you!*"

Her feet stayed rooted. To buy time, I rocked back.

Everyone stared.

She moved with me.

"Ha! Too much good *blong*, Abigail!" her friend whooped.

My body kept the dance position, and we moved.

"This is 'the frame', Abigail. My left pushes your right hand. That signals you to move back. Keep your hand pushing against mine."

Slowly, she felt my motion and moved with me. Her pals hooted. But we kept dancing.

By sundown, I had three couples and was teaching basic foxtrot.

The couples tired and sat on the floor to rest. Chairs seemed called for.

"How you *staap*, lifesaver?" Wyne asked from the Quonset doorway.

A group clustered behind him. His jaws worked, chewing something. Red froth stained his lips.

"Him ate de betel nut!" one of my men students said.

"Sign must be, prohibit dat *ting* dere."

"Dis fella here, *blong* him save me life!" Wyne said, slurring his words. Maybe he was high, on the betel nut or something else.

"Mister Wyne, please," I said. Trying to play the modest hero might work my scheme.

"He did! He did!" Wyne said.

"Local ladies act shy," I said.

"Need a tourist woman as a hostess," I said. "Someone told me, a foreign lady staying at the club. Wonder where she is."

"I find out," Wyne said.

"They, *garem*, all *tok-tok* me. Respect my age."

CHAPTER TWENTY FOUR

Raising A Mess
or
Dance Fussin'

"Everyone dance it up!" I hollered. "Everyone tells me that Guadalcanal folks, right here in Honiara City, are the best dancers in the Pacific."

Nobody seemed to get it.

"Feel like P.T. Barnum here," I muttered to myself. "Trying to sell Busto Private Parts Love Potion to the simple, trusting island natives here."

The men, some in their sixties like me, shuffled towards the wide-hipped women in sarongs.

"Younger ones here, boss?" demanded a character with a pointy beard and blue tattoos on his meaty arms. He pushed his beard forward as he talked. "Dem *BLONG* grandmas."

"You don't get it. In Ballroom, everyone dances with the world. It is democracy."

"Wass?"

"Maybe that's the wrong word. Democracy not too popular in this civil war you got here. But dancers dance. We men don't just ask the young and the beautiful to dance. We should find the nervous, timid woman, no longer young, who comes in along, clutching her handbag –"

"Wass you *tok-tok*?"

"You're right. I'm gassing too much. Talking over my audience. In Ballroom, you don't window-shop for some beauty to help you fix up your life's problems. You just dance. And, sometimes, you watch your dance partner skip back to the earlier, happier years when everything was fun."

"Bull," he said.

He walked away.

"Well, that's one word that ain't Solomon Islands Pidgin," I said. "I can sure understand that word 'bull'. That fella thinks that Ballroom is a Manhattan singles bar, hunting out the runway models. He just doesn't get it."

The radio gods smiled upon me as good dance songs kept flowing out onto our dance floor.

Elie the barmaid from the Yacht Club showed up in the doorway. She looked excited and breathless tonight. Something stirred me in watching her.

HEY, HEY, WHAT IS THIS? I asked myself.

BETTER NOT, my inner Good Angel whispered. YOU'RE HERE TO FIND YOUR DAUGHTER.

Pointy Beard practically turned an ankle crossing the floor to take Elie's arm for a dance.

"No grabbing, Pointy," I said. "In Ballroom, we only grab when the partner asks us to. A few times, that is."

Elie smiled at him, pretty as a cameo, and shook her head in a refusal. That did not sit well with Pointy. He kept holding her.

With another smile, she twisted her wrist in a delicate turn, broke his grip and stepped away from him.

"Barmaid experience wins again," I said.

Wyne danced past me with a full-faced Black woman with a blonde lock of hair near the left temple.

"Max, this Salty," Wyne said. "She blonde. That cause one you *Jumbles* in her family long ago. Call dem 'Salt-heads' here."

"My pleasure, Ms. Salty. Are you enjoying the dance?"

"How you *staaap*?" she asked.

"I'm in my element," I said. "Mr. Wyne, remember what we discussed?"

"Dat Yank gal?"

"Yes."

Ms. Salty gurgled out some Pidgin, too fast for me to follow.

"Mister Wyne, you're my interpreter in this foreign land of Guadalcanal, where everyone speaks English," I said. "Technically."

Wyne smirked and squired Ms. Salty into a dip move, to feel her body against his.

Taking a woman partner who seemed alone, I lost myself in another foxtrot, cha-cha and something local that passed for a rhumba.

Trying to look nonchalant, I stepped towards Elie.

"You're looking happy tonight," formed my suave opening line.

"Yaas," she said, paying me no mind. "These *wantoks* dance and get thirsty. Won't do. It just won't do."

"Quite," I said, mocking the British.

"So, I bring you whiskey bottle," she said.

That made me beam.

"So, you really care," I stammered.

"I care 'bout twenty dollars. American. Not Solomon Island dollars. Must replace it tomorrow. Tell boss it got broken."

"What kind of bust-head giggle water are you trying to dump on me?"

"Cradle Mountain Malt Whisky from Tasmania."

"Should have quite a kick," I said.

"Yes or no? In my shoulder bag now."

"You know, Elie, you're getting modern right before my eyes. Here's the Yankee cash. You want to hold it up to a strong light, make sure it's not my picture on it?"

"Is not. Who is, this Jackson?"

"Jackson knew his whiskey, all right. Nasty, quick-tempered duelist who owned 300 Black slaves and fought against freedom for them."

"You make him leader, on your money?"

"I wasn't consulted."

Across the floor, the Pointy shoved another man. It looked like he meant it.

"That's a real shove," I said. "Real beer."

Pointy barked as fists flew, and women screamed..

CHAPTER TWENTY FIVE

Chat
or
Battle

"Trouble right here," I hissed. "Right here in Dancing City,"

Pointy punched his pal again. I saw the lip spurt blood. Ms. Salty, the dancer, slugged Pointy. He kicked her. She grabbed his shoulders and slammed him back into the tin wall.

Shoving dancers aside, I reached Pointy. My body set, boxer-style. He swung another haymaker at me. Being set, I bobbed to the outside of it. His right hand grazed my left ear. I skittered back.

My dancers split away from me to watch. Some still held their partners in dance position. That felt good. Maybe my example were taking root.

Striking him was out. Guadalcanal's only dance teacher must win the crowd.

"Hey, *wantok*," I said, trying not to pant. Hopping across the hut winded me. "What you wanna do, man?"

He punched out again, a flurry. I stepped to my right and back. His punches missed. I was too far away. My nerves screamed. All of me wanted to kick his thigh, elbow his jaw and chop his neck until he dropped. That was wise combat. Trying to talk him down was not.

"Do him up, mon!" a man shouted. That confused me. Who was he rooting for? Pointy came closer. I faked a step left. He threw another, I went under it and shoved him backwards.

"All jokin' aside," I tried saying in a calm, wise voice, the tolerant veteran. "Shouldn't we be dancing, instead of play-acting like this?"

"Put your hands on me, *waytii mann?*" Pointy ground out. "Bust you up."

I let my face show surprise.

"What for?" I asked.

"We just having a bit of fun. Nothing worth much."

Fighting over insults always seemed murderously stupid to me. Now, I had to play it off like we were teenagers again.

"Dancing and funning around like this makes me thirsty," I announced. "So, who wants some free whiskey? I'm gonna have a drink."

Then I turned my back on Pointy and stepped towards Elie, with a fake smile on my lips.

"Hey, you!" Pointy hollered. "*Waytii mann!*"

"I been married, Pointy," I whispered. "I know how to ignore."

Elie had already uncapped the Cradle Mountain Malt Whisky from her bag and shuffled out a bank of shot glasses from her purse. She clinked the shot glasses down on a folding card table, like a saloon gal in a cowboy movie. Her body clenched inside her dress.

"Men are paying you attention, Elie," I said. "And they always will. Guadalcanal is an island of polygamists."

My scheme exploded.

Pointy moved fast for a sloppy big man. He clapped a hand on my shoulder and spun me around. His right came up for the punch.

"Half a mo, Claude," Wyne said. "Stop cuttin' de fool. Why you always gotta be Peck's bad boy?"

"Old fool –"

"*Nao gud tok-tok!*" another local, with tribal gashes on both cheeks and red feathers stuck to his belt, said. "Respect *himfella.*"

"Why for?" Pointy said. "*Hem wiff wayti man.*"

"Yu *blong waytii mann* same-same *hem*," the Red Feathers said. "Show right, hem."

"Yeah," I said. "Whatever he said."

Pointy made an ugly face at me and stalked away.

"You *blong* hit hem," Wyne said. "Know you not afraid, hem. You save *mifella* life."

"Told you, another guy saved you," I said.

"You the right Johnnie. Me *tok-tok* everyone. *Garem.* Dem *tok-tok olketa.*"

The Cradle Mountain Malt Whisky burned my throat on the way down and tickled the gizzards.

"Where you move like dat, boxer stuff?" Ms. Salty queried.

"I could ask you the same thing, Ms. Salty. That was a good right hand you belted old Pointy with. Where'd you learn that?"

"Five boys, my mama and papa have."

"Claude 'Pointy', he gone," the Red Feather man said.

Elie took away the shot glass after I drained it.

"Elie, thanks for keeping things cool," I said.

She mumbled something and walked over to a group of dancers lined up by the empty shot glasses on the table. The Cradle Mountain bottle stayed in her hand.

"Our Hero is not doing well with the Fair Maiden," I said to anyone nearby who might hear and understand. My dancers were now drinking.

The radio pumped out Muzak now, and some of them danced to it, alone or with partners. Pointy's punches gave them something to gab about.

"He gone come back *nao gud,*" a large woman in a blue jean dress with silver conchos on the hips said. "He like bother us."

"Him papa, same same," her friend put in, fanning herself with a rice-paper fan in tonight's sticky heat.

Wyne escorted another woman back to me. She wore a flowered print dress and necklaces of iridescent sea-shells over her breasts.

"She tell me," Wyne said.

"You ask about dat Yank gal from the hotel?" she asked.

"She go by Jimmy boat, to Marau Island. Far, far from here, mon."

CHAPTER TWENTY SIX

Next Place
or
The Enchanted Island

"What island are you talking about?" I asked.

"Marau Island," Wyne said. "Me never been. Kakamoras live Marau."

"Kakamoras? What's that?"

"Silly *tok-tok*. Stories for scare *pikannini* babes."

Everyone crowded near us. Dancing and watching Pointy attack me got them talking.

"*Hemi* little fella, Kakamora," Ms. Salty said.

"I got it," I said. "'*Hemi*' is Pidgin for the word 'him'. "

"Live in caves," she said. "Long hair, dirty. Speak funny lingo."

"Are you telling me true?" I asked. "Or, are you just playing Pin-the-tale-on-the-Honky?"

"Some us fella see dem," Wyne said. "In Weather Coast, jungle grow, cover everything, not many fella be there, say Kakamoras live. Marau Island *tok-tok* same ting, Johnnie."

"Kinda like Melanesian leprechauns," I said. "But not so clean. What's the Weather Coast?"

"Hemi south coast, Guadalcanal. Nao road. Nao leaf path. Jump from place to new place, walk Weather Coast."

"They fellas *blong* Marau," another woman with round staring eyes set in a weathered face insisted. "Eat men."

They crowded around. Some drank. Everyone wanted to sling words.

"Cannibals," Ms. Salty said.

"No *moa*, now," Wyne said. "Too modern. Huh? Can't be."

"Might be," I said. "Cannibals, I mean. That's why there's a word for it."

"Marau fellas, no speak English," Wyne said.

"That never bothers a New Yorker," I said. "Most jokers in restaurants back home don't, either."

"Prim-it-tive," Wyne said.

"Look around you here," I said. "This isn't exactly Harvard Yard."

"Lotta malaria there," he said.

"Correct me if I'm wrong," I said. "Nothing prevents malaria and there's no cure, either. Without treatment, it can settle your hash. Permanent."

"Settle what?"

"Sorry. I mean it can kill you. Pills can knock down your chances of getting it, both before and after your exposure to it. Mosquitoes carry it and sting you. Right?"

"Dey one way, not catch malaria," Wyne said.

"Yeah, I know. Bypass Guadalcanal."

"Some Marau Johnnies, been missionary school, *tok-tok* English," Ms. Salty said. "Others, *tok-tok* Are-Are lingo from Malaita."

"Why do folks living on Guadalcanal Island speak the language from Malaita?" I asked.

Wyne shook his head.

"Prim-it-tive," he repeated.

"Why we poor," Ms. Salty said.

"Old time fellas, *blong* cavemen time, they live Marau," Wyne said. "Maybe Yank gal wanna lookim caves."

"Or maybe somebody took her," I said.

"*Wass?*"

"Never mind. How can I fly to Marau Island?"

"Not fly, Johnnie. *Hemi* got *nao* airstrip. Eighty miles here."

"Bus? Jeep for hire?"

"Dey no roads, Johnnie. Just leaf trails. Walk *hemi*."

"Captain Jimmy boat!" Elie said. She had joined our group without me noticing. Something seemed to excite her. Her teeth and eyes flashed. She was looking different, more fresh and lively, now. Maybe the fight had stirred her like the others.

"*Hemi* go every Tuesday."

"What day is today?" I asked. "Lost track, in this island paradise."

"Today Tuesday. He go at ten tonight."

"Almost ten now," Wyne said. He flashed a tinny wristwatch with a chipped ceramic British Union Jack on it.

"Next boat?" I asked.

"Next Tuesday."

"Text Captain Jimmy that I'm his newest passenger," I said.

"Text?" Ms. Salty asked. Her face formed a question.

"My mistake," I said. "Again. Phone him."

"*Hemi* don't got Solomon Islands Telekom phone," Elie said.

"How come you know so much *hemi*?" Ms. Salty asked. "You *hemi* secret sweetie?"

"No time to pack," I said. "From what you all tell me, Marau is in worse shape for dance than anywhere in Guadalcanal. Island seems to need a dance teacher like me very bad. So, I better get there."

They needed a reason for me rocketing away like this.

"Gotta start island-hopping, my dears," I said. "Elie, please hold my stuff and rent out my room. Just me and my cane. Going to Marau Island."

Everyone laughed.

"You crazy and rich, can do *olketa*, everything," Ms. Salty said.

"This trip makes me famous?"

"Before you teach dem dance, they Johnnies eat you," Ms. Salty said.

"*Dat* racist *tok-tok*," Wyne said.

CHAPTER TWENTY SEVEN

To A Far Place
or
If I Survive

My dancers brought me from our Quonset hut towards the murky water near the Yacht Club.

"This feels like a college panty raid when everyone's hammered-down drunk and not making sense," I said. "But a lot of fun."

"We're playing with our dance teacher," Elie said. She was talking proper English speech now. She might slip back to island Pidgin at any time.

"I can smell the whiskey breath mixed with perfume and your local soap," I told Elie.

"You say we *wantoks* smell bad?" she asked. Her voice raised up.

"No," I said. "Was ever a man more misunderstood? That might have been the only soap sold here and I'm starting to recognize it. Smells good."

Her eyes held mine.

"Your perfume is wonderful," I said.

She snorted something in Pidgin.

"Elie, I hope you ain't talking nasty about me," I said.

"Don't call me 'Elie,'" she said. "That my government name. On paper. Licenses. No *Jumble* can say me real name, *blong* me."

"Then, what is your real name?"

"American Merchant Marine man give me a nickname. 'cause I was love him a lot. Everywhere. Everything. Understand?"

"I'm trying to. What was the name?"

"Gaffme."

"Gaffme? One word or two?"

"No matter," she said.

"Yes, I'm afraid it does. The word gaff is fisherman talk. You shouldn't call yourself by that name. It's disrespectful. A gaff is a pointed spear to stab into a fish –"

"Mi savvy gaff!" she hissed.

"Okay, then. But I won't call you Gaffme. To me, you are Elie, my friend and guide."

"You're a silly man. Make a lot of bother that way."

She wheeled around, using her hips and dropped back into the crowd.

The beach lay dark in the half-light.

"This is the Pacific?" I asked Ms. Salty.

"Nao. This just Point Cruz. So many Jap, Yank, Aussie ships dead here, call it 'Ironbottom Sound'. No Johnnie can pull up the dead boats *blong* here."

"There's no boat here," I said.

My fingers walked up my sword cane to the release catch.

"Maybe you happy-go-lucky dancers playing a trick to rip off this eccentric Yank millionaire."

"Pardon?"

"Know I'll never understand the Third World," I went on. "'cause I'm a White Johnnie, Manhattan-born. Everyone here needs cash."

"Yaas," Elie said. "But we no steal."

"Then, where's this boat?"

"*Hemi* boat," she said.

Behind a tree grove ashore, a white bulge about forty-feet long bobbed on the water. The trees had hidden it. It was running without lights. Flashlights bobbed on the deck.

"Elie," I said. "Can you tell me –"

She was gone, back into the bush somewhere.

My face burned and I could feel it.

"Dumb White preppy," I cussed myself.

My carefree group was fading back into the shadows, where Elie had gone.

"Hey," I said. "Did you hear me? I was just joshing, you know."

Nobody answered. Wyne, Ms. Salty and the dancers kept moving away, back towards the road and away from the beach.

Then, they were gone and I was left alone near the boat.

"Maybe they got no sense of humor," I said. "Gotta remember that I'm not pounding down Singapore Slings at the Comic Strip Comedy Club on Second Avenue back home."

"Git away boat!" a man shouted in accented bad English from the stern.

Lifting both hands, I stood my ground.

"Go!" he shouted.

For years, I had shipped out overseas and tonight recalled the culture.

"Captain!" I hollered. "Talk with Captain!"

A gun blasted.

CHAPTER TWENTY EIGHT

Dickering
or
Fair Market Price

By reflex, I hit the dirt.

My bruises hurt.

A wide Asian man leaned over the ship's rail.

"You very shy boy!" he shouted. The voice swung high and scratchy. He sounded like a drinker. "Stand up to see!"

He held something tight against his hip. It could be a gun. I stayed behind some stunted trees.

"What you want?" he giggled out in my direction.

"Captain."

"Why? Captain fat old fool. Worthless."

"I want to give him some money."

"Good for you. Captain like money."

Recalling old cowboy films, I dug up a rock at my feet and tossed it at the boat. It hit the cabin ten feet from him.

He turned. His hand sparked orange and kicked upwards. The flame showed a thick metal gun in his mitt, braced against his gut. The hammer clicked back.

Gun smoke wafted near his face.

Excited voices shouted in some language. I had no clue.

His gun looked like a monstrous clown cap pistol. It had a fat cylinder and a curved handle that I could see in this half-light.

"Why money?" he shouted.

"Want to reach Marau Island."

"Whuffor?"

"Wanna teach Ballroom Dancing."

"Go, whistle for it."

"Ah, British talk," I said. "You Hong Kong Chinese?"

"I not from nowhere, *Laal Gand.* You gone teach dance dem boys, HAH!" He spat out the word.

"Where they been hiding you, pal?" I asked.

"HUH?"

"I said that I will pay good money. Marau Island. What do you want?"

"Not gonna take you."

"Five hundred dollars American, like me American."

"You got him now?"

"You gonna shoot me for it?"

"Maybe."

"I like an honest man. Permission to board, sir?"

"Guess so, *Laal Gand.*"

Instead of twirling the cane, I gripped it in my left and let my right hand fingers splay over the carved handle, ready to draw the blade. Maybe I should have practiced more pulling it out and stabbing because right now it felt awkward.

The gangplank swayed under my bulk.

The man's wide face with a gap- toothed smile showed some gold front teeth. He had the kind of face that looked like it was always smiling, like a panda.

His hair was black as tar but age-lines showed along his mouth and chin. He could have been anywhere from forty-five to seventy years old.

"Sir, could we stow the gun? Normally, I wouldn't care but I'm pregnant right now and don't want the child born with phobias."

"What gun?"

"Don't point it, please. That gun. Never saw one like that. That Chinese?"

"Naw, from you crazy Yanks. Your Confederate Rebel cavalry, Civil War. Is nine shots of .44 caliber. Barrel underneath here shoots buckshot. You choice. Heavy gun but she very sweet, good girl. You Yanks make replica like this one."

"You don't need it with me. Peaceful rich type."

"That good. Five hundred. Now. My hand."

"What about the captain?"

He giggled.

"I captain," he guffawed. "Only bang-bang gun on boat. No good trash crew, sons of unclean mothers, yes, please Jesus, your worship."

"Captain, here's the money. What's your name, sir?"

"Captain."

"Kind of stuffy talk that hurts my bruises. I'm Max, your dance teacher. Would your crew like to learn Argentine tango? It might civilize them some. You're Captain Jimmy?"

"Only English call me Jimmy. Mrugank, my name."

"You Chinese?"

"I not from nowhere, *Laal Gand*. Burma, India, what the hell, okay? Money okay. We get underway, three shakes, lamb's tail, okay?"

"Think I understand your Latin, Captain. You look like an important man with many connections. Anybody on Marau Island I can pay for a bed and food?"

"Bloody hell everyone. We *tok-tok blong* Marau."

"AND you speak the King's Pidgin, Captain. That's nice to hear."

"You have a kip anywhere, on deck."

"Sure, Captain. When in doubt, nap."

From the trees ashore, I saw movement. The Captain shouted. Someone on board shone a spotlight into the bush ashore.

The light showed my dancers moving into their own steps. Wyne extended both arms to Ms. Salty while the others chanted. Ms. Salty turned and stopped. She put her hand on her hip and looked backwards over her shoulder, like a coquette daring a suitor to flirt with her.

"*Affa raffa, jinga thissa boo too!*" they chanted.

That's what it sounded like to me.

On the boat, the crewmen clapped, guffawed and whistled.

"Max! Max!" Ms. Salty shouted and she twirled her body, bent at the waist and pointed her bottom at the boat.

"Am I being praised with faint damnation or damned with faint praise?" I queried.

Others joined in the dance. They pirouetted and jetted. Heads bobbed. They formed what looked like a moving conga line and danced into the bush.

CHAPTER TWENTY NINE

Voyage
or
Wrong Time To Get Seasick

In the darkness along the boat, I found a deck chair and folded myself into it.

Moving woke me.

The boat was pulling away from shore and the diesel smell flowed in the air.

"We go!" the Captain crowed. He stepped along the deck.

"Why a night run, Captain? Don't you need the daylight to see wrecks and such here in this Ironbottom Sound?"

"Daylight, terrs shoot. Please, no, Jesus Christ, your worship."

"Terrs?"

"Terrorists."

"Which terrorists?"

"I damn't care. Bullets hit my boat, my crew, body, crap! Night, they not watching. Better chance. Stop cars on road, easy."

"Night is more dangerous, Captain."

"Got good watch, lamp. Okay, no sweat, GI. Maybe drunken terrorist bums sleep."

We watched the dark shoreline.

Shots cracked.

I hit the deck faster than the good Captain.

"Maybe drunken terrorist bums not asleep," I said.

He cursed in a foreign tongue.

More shots fired.

"No light, please, Jesus, your worship!" the Captain wailed.

Our spotlight doused.

Fear froze me fast. Any rifle bullet could reach me and cripple me. Or worse.

"You know my name!" he shouted. He leaned over the gunwale and cupped big hands. "This Captain Jimmy! You make trouble for me, my boat, shoot, you son-of-a-gun and I mess you up like dead pig! Dogs defile your mother upside down in rickshaw!"

Another shot fired.

"Sounds like a shotgun but my memories are fuzzy," I said. "Once, I thought that I was shotgunned by a baby firecracker."

"No matter!"

He drew the enormous pistol, stuck it over the rail and triggered three shots. It bucked and plumed fire in his hand.

This close, it stung my ears. Tomorrow, the ears would buzz. If there was a tomorrow.

"See Guadalcanal and die," I whispered.

More shots came from farther down the coast. Some pinged into our hull.

"Go back to Malaita!" some gunny fool ashore hollered. "You not born here!"

"Me, neither," I said. "Does that mean I can I go now?"

"Ugi gonna ethnic clean Guadalcanal," the fool cawed. "You see!"

Pidgin talk ripped out from shore.

"Stop these damn engines, please, Jesus, your worship!" the Captain shouted.

"Seems like you invoke the Deity in all matters," I said.

"We turn about, head back Honiara!" he shouted.

"Why all the way?" I said. "Just get out of rifle range."

"I captain! Not you, damn *Laal Gand* Yank! We go where I say!"

Guns kept cracking.

"You hurt my feelings, Cap," I said aloud. "It doesn't matter that some rascals trying to kill us both. My feelings come first. Don't ask me why. Just my delicate nature."

"Talk crazy, *Laal Gand.*"

"I don't know you well enough to start a feud, Cap. You the boss." He grabbed my bicep with one mitt. The gun waved.

"Damn't trust my own crew!" he hissed. "Some from Guadalcanal, some from Malaita. Might mutiny me, take me to torture place. Keep in the middle, always quiet, damnit!"

"So, what's your plan?"

"Trust you, *Laal Gand* –"

"Wait a second," I said. "What does '*Laal Gand*' mean?"

"In Hindi, that is 'Red Ass.' What we call you Whites. Cause when we get our bottoms *blong* us we get darker, our skin. Yufellas, you sunburn, you skin get red. So, in India, call you 'Red-Ass'. '*Laal Gand.*'"

More shots fired. They were farther away now.

"Trust you, you not Guadalcanal or Malaita boy. Damn't care, this piggish damn dumb bollocks."

"Well, I never," I said. "Racial profiling rears its ugly head."

"*Yufella* wanna *tok-tok* this stuff, they shooting at us?"

"You're right, Cap. Later for this."

We drifted farther from shore. The shots stopped. Our anchor chained and dropped.

"We behind wreck of Jap ship now," the Captain said. "Nobody ashore see us, shoot. Nothing."

The crew, mostly Blacks and some who looked South Asian swaggered onto the deck, shouting in Pidgin and in a dozen languages that I had never heard before.

"Timor, Sarawak, Borneo, Papuan New Guinea," the Captain said. "All different sons of guns, on my damn boat."

Tobacco and sweetish clove cigarettes lit. Some puffed broken cigars, holding fingers over the gaps in the leaf.

"Here is bag some crazy English left here," the Captain said. "Use for sleep. Clothes inside."

I peered into the leftover luggage.

"And books," I said. "One about Guadalcanal war. About time I learned something about it."

"You can read, take this flashlight?"

"This year, yes."

"Damn't like books. Like nature. You read all night, and get tired, no can work tomorrow."

"Yes, I can. But I'm gonna finish this book."

The boat rolled as I read. The crew gawked at me. The book kept turning pages under my hand. Sleep came, and I slipped into a dream.

CHAPTER THIRTY

Last Night I Had the Craziest
or
Unbelievable

As I lay sprawled on the boat deck, the Guadalcanal war book open on my gut, I dreamed a dream that the history book had plagued me with.

●

August 7, 1942
Somewhere in the South Pacific
"Get down that cargo net, boot!" Someone shouted at me. "Or else, you too fricking young, be in this man's Marine Corps!"

"Maybe I am," I muttered.

Nobody could hear me. Muttering disrespect was one of the tricks Parris Island boot camp had taught me.

My Springfield '03 rifle slid and barked skin off my neck. It stung.

"Watch out where you put your fat fingers, ya re-tard!" another Marine shouted.

"Stow it!"

"Jarheads getting the shakes, start with the invasion nerves talk," our Sarge said. "Suck it up, buttercup."

By now, we were inside the landing craft.

Just like before a big ball game, my nerves made time fly.

"Remember, you got ten days ammo for your Springfield," the Sarge said. "Fifty rounds. Don't waste 'em, Japs slice you with Samurai stickers."

My hands shook on my rifle. Sarge saw it.

"Right, Royster?" he asked me.

"Aye aye, Sarge," I said. My voice cracked.

Marines stared at me, then looked away.

"Weak sister," someone mumbled.

I felt bad.

Breakfast of coffee, eggs and biscuits roiled in my gut.

"Sarge, what's the poop on this Guadal-thing-a-mah-jing place?" a hefty guy with a scarred face asked, jaws working some tobacco.

"Nobody knows nothing from nothing about this dump, this Guadalcanal," the Sarge said.

He smelled of gun oil and old sweat.

"Our first landing fighting Japs and none of us knows jungle fighting or anything else 'bout staying alive there. Corps been cut and raped by sissy politicians to save dough."

"Wasn't gonna be no war," the tobacco chewer said. "Now, Japs wanna whole world, make us slaves."

"Here's the beach!" Sarge shouted. "Go, Marines!"

BAM! Everything blew. Water hit us.

"Jump off!" someone bellowed.

I jumped.

Bodies hit me. I went down in warm water. Another big body pushed me under. My breath went out. I choked. A combat boot hit my lip. The lip split.

I broke surface.

"Dad!" I shouted. "Where you?"

"Get out my way!" a voice hollered too loud in my ear.

Sarge floated past, bleeding. His eyes fluttered. They shut.

"Sarge!" I shouted. "My weapon's gone!"

"So's Sarge," Corporal Tex said. "Where's your piece?"

Shots hit from the shore.

"I DON'T KNOW!" I screamed.

"Pipe down," Tex said.

He could command.

"Take my musette bag."

He tossed it to me.

It was a heavy shoulder pouch, a foot square, Marine Corps green, like our dungarees.

"I need my rifle!" I shouted.

"Get you one later," he said. "Just wade ashore."

"Tex, I don't need your gear!"

"Don't take it, the Japs'll getya!" he said.

"Stop jawing, you two!" someone shouted. "Japs ain't waiting!"

We went ashore.

My wet greens oozed water. Tex's bag swung wild on my shoulder.

Palm trees and foliage lay ahead. Gunfire splashed orange bursts. Oil smell and smoke covered us.

"I'm going in deeper!" I shouted.

Behind me, my landing craft burned. I needed to flee.

"No dice, kid!" Tex shouted. "Stay close!"

I broke and ran ahead.

Fear was making me sick. Nobody would see me hurl breakfast here in the jungle.

Jungle vines whipped my cheek.

Nobody could see me now.

Tex's bag held a clunky shotgun, sawn down about ten inches. Oiled double barrels shone. Red shells rattled. A cowboy Colt pistol with ivory grips and a short barrel lay alongside. A Longhorn steer decorated the grips.

"Tex give me his hideout guns," I said. "Stuff the Corps outlaws."

Brush covered me.

A brown arm hit my face. I rocked back and swung my mitts out. The Musette bag dropped. My punch hit. Another arm grabbed my wrist. I spun down swinging. A Jap face showed blood. I jabbed his jaw.

CHAPTER THIRTY ONE

Meeting the Enemy
or
Propaganda Looks Wrong

My dream kept unreeling. Later, I remembered this much.

●

I kept throwing jabs at the Jap.

"Give it up, Tokyo!" I hissed.

He dodged my punches I could not seem to hit him.

"Stop this," he said in thick English.

"You savvy?"

Maybe I was copying Tarzan movies again.

"I speak. I professional Rikusental Marine paratrooper. Like you."

That was stretching it. I was a fool kid who signed a paper. He was a pro.

He kept moving under my punches.

I threw a right.

He blocked it. He hit my throat. Same hand. I gagged and jabbed my left.

He dodged that and hit me on the forearm, armpit and spine. He used his hand sideways. It hurt.

I wheeled around and threw a sucker right haymaker.

He stopped it, grabbed my wrist and stepped forward. My arm twisted. He kicked my foot back. I flew forward and lit on my chin. The ground slammed into me. My eyes closed.

"Jujitsu beats boxing," my Sarge said.

"Hey, Sarge," I said. "Howya doin? Jap here got me. Wanna shoot the breeze?"

Stunned, I could see my Sarge, the jagged teeth, rough, pock-marked face, droopy brown eyes.

Sarge shook his head.

"No more shooting the breeze," he said. "Not no more."

His Minnesota accent grated like always to my New York ears.

"'sides which," Sarge said. "I'm dead, ya know."

Sarge folded up as flames covered his body. He looked like something made of paper-mache. Somehow, I had lost my Marine Corps greens and wore my corduroy red and blue cowboy shirt with the white fake pearl snap buttons. It was the same shirt I wore in Manhattan, teaching my dance class on the East River. It seemed like years ago now.

Behind the burning Sarge, rows of Marines in their dress blues lined up. Their leather gleamed like wet black tar, against the cream of their dress gloves and the belts cinching narrow waists. The scarlet and gold chevrons caught the light. The mameluke dress swords, designed after the Tripoli pirate scimitar, dangled on their hips. Short hair and bony boy faces stayed above the golden globe-and-anchor choker collar jewels.

Hundreds sang, deep and husky, "From the Halls of Mon-te-zuma To the shores of Tripoli!"

Behind them, cannons boomed.

The Marines caught fire from the Sarge. They lit orange flames and then smoldered to black and charcoal ash. The white hats melted. To their left, beautiful Melanesian women wept.

"Who will save us now?" Elie wailed.

A Jap caught Elie, stripped her naked and mounted her from the rear.

"Stop!" she screamed. "I am not animal! Why you make love to me this bad way?"

My eyes cleared up.

The Jap stood over me. He looked different from the Hearst paper propaganda cartoons. The cartoons showed li'l round jokers with buck teeth, Coke-bottle specs and evil faces. This fella looked lanky and angled, standing just a couple of inches under my six feet. His black hair was crew cut and he sported a long horse face with deep lines from the weather cut into his skin.

"You tied up, stop you from get killed," he said. "Hate war. Sick of it."

"Lemme go, please!"

My own crying shocked me.

"Ahhh," he said. "When men stop shooting, I take you to our camp. Prison okay for you. No more war. You Americans lose this airfield and we take it back. Our planes fly here, bomb your ships, bomb Australia and land us Marines on that coast. Before this, the stupid war, I study like officer. History, tactics. Australia too big to defend. We get in somewhere, cut defenders off from others. You have only planes from carriers. We have Guadalcanal airfield. Nothing can stop us."

"Huh?" I asked.

"No. We can't beat you now. You too much industrial. Strong. But we can make you want, leave us alone and fight Germans in Europe. You thousands miles away. What you care Pacific island? America should fight Europe war. We got airplane. We hurt engine to make big noise, stop you from sleep. You Marines know this plane already from Wake Island fight. Call this plane 'Washing Machine Charley.' Tired Marines cannot fight us."

I strained to say something tough, like a seasoned veteran in the movies might say.

"Tell it to the Marines," I croaked.

"Yours or mine? You want make slaves, we yellow people. Took Asia for your banks. Drugs. I study. Japan free Asia from you. No more war."

"Then why'd you join?"

My hard-boiled act did not work. I was crying again.

"Don't join, Kemp-ei Tai, secret police take me. Family disgrace. Force into army same-same. Sent punishment group, get killed by bandits, China, somewhere. I see many young men, yours and mine, dead tomorrow."

CHAPTER THIRTY TWO

Waking
or
Laura Nyro Sings

The boat moving woke me up from my dream.

"Wow," I mumbled, broken-mouth and drooly in the jowls. "That was some dream." I was still stretched out on the deck. The Captain sat nearby, smoking a greenish-brown cigar in this heat. The sun was coming up, painting the dark jungle shoreline with daylight.

"Can't believe that Guadalcanal could hand me a nightmare like that," I said.

"Huh?" the Captain said. "Huh? Huh?"

"That question could grow annoying," I said.

"Terrorists shoot at you, make you nightmare."

"Right. I never joined the Marines before. Captain, what's your real name? What you were born?"

"Huh, huh?"

"Please."

"Mrugank. That my family call me."

"What does the name mean?"

"Lion."

"Then you must be brave like a lion," I said. "Brave enough to keep sailing along the north coast here and get me to Marau Island by tonight."

A shot fired.

"Huh? Maybe. But you gotta remember, I the Captain. Like in your Laura Nyro songs."

"What is a Laura Nyro?"

"Where you born, America?"

"New Yorker. For life."

"Laura Nyro, too. Huh? Brit music man play me CDs. Best singer, the world."

"Don't know her. Can she stop these bullets? Could we maybe talk about her later, maybe? After these shots?"

"She write song, 'Eli's Comin', 'Stone Soul Picnic,' and 'Wedding Bell Blues'. How can you not know?"

"Shipped out overseas sometimes. Gets you out of the mainstream."

I was lying. I knew all about Laura Nyro. But I wanted to hustle the Captain, to make him keep talking and sailing to Marau. My scheme scared me. If he figured that I was lying, he would hurt me.

"Listen. Huh?"

He took out a beat-up i-Phone and thumbed a button.

Far away, shots fired.

A woman's voice flowed from the phone.

Piano music came, urgent, then rhythmic.

It made my feet twitch, wanting to dance.

"You hear?" Captain Mrugank said. "Is song 'Captain for Dark Mornings.' She often sing about the Captain. Listen."

He played another song.

"This song," he said, "called 'Captain Saint Lucifer'. You see?"

"So, if I get right what you're trying to say," I said, "the Captain is the mystery figure. Is the Captain her father, boyfriend, lover, ex dominating lover who will destroy her? Nobody knows. But he is always standing there. Not talking?"

"No. He never talk."

This Captain needed his ego boosted, so that I could con him into doing what I wanted.

"Thank you for playing those Laura Nyro songs," I said. "You're right about her voice. It's wonderful."

That took a bit to sink in.

"She is dead young, long time ago," he said. Getting him melancholy would not help me.

"That's okay, Captain," I said. "Like you say, you're the Captain here on your boat, just like that other captain in her songs. Those tunes will last forever. And I'm going to buy her music. And I'll have these local folks dancing to it as soon as I can."

"Dance to her songs?"

"Hell, Captain. We can use your phone and Laura Nyro's music for our first Marau Island dance class. But we've got to get there first. And alive."

"Laura Nyro," he said. "And I her Captain."

"Maybe you're a bit hipped on her yourself, Cap."

He did not hear me. He brandished the phone and showed me the album photo. The photo was a young White woman with a pale face with heavy black hair and brows. Her face looked intense and calm at the same time. Her brown eyes looked into me.

"You see, you see?" he shouted above the slap of water against the boat's hull. He needed calming down.

"Yes, Captain. I see."

Distraction might work.

"Where are we heading now?" I asked.

"Mataniku River. Safe now. This is Kukum area. You Marines shoot Japs here. Big battle –"

"Could we leave the Marines somewhere else now, Captain? They bring me nightmares. Why does everyone here on Guadalcanal talk about the war so much? It's over now. Japan is friendly."

"Not ever. We remember. War big stuff."

"Now, you got a civil war. Do something about that."

We glided upriver now. It looked spooky.

"You dunno nothing."

"Guadalcanal reminds me of my whiskey drinking days in Tombstone, Arizona. The town too tough to die, they called it. Everyone there seemed to be a part-time historian and a full-time drunk. They could handle the past with ease. But not the present."

"I no drink."

"Probably a good thing. Else, you'd be mooning drunk over the Japanese and Laura Nyro."

"Laura die long ago. Forty-nine years old. She got the cancer. But, forget this thing. Make me sad. Japs fight Marines here at Mataniku River. They both want airstrip. Control airstrip –"

"-You control the Pacific. I got that. And, if you snag the Pacific, you got the war."

"Japs cross Mataniku right here. 7,000 Japs. You Marines charge them. Bayonet charge. Many die. You should know all this –"

Shots hit our boat.

CHAPTER THIRTY THREE

We Interrupt This Laura Nyro
or
Jungle Fighting

"We go up Mataniku," the Captain said. "Safer there."

The Mataniku River spanned about forty feet across, with fringes of tall palm trees along the shore. In the light now, the water looked gunmetal colored.

"Doesn't appear too healthy, that water," I said.

"Malaita kids use for water closet," the Captain said. "Bog. You know. Toilet."

"Political statement. How d'you know the kids are from Malaita?"

"Smell."

"More politics. The ones shooting at us, which side are they on?"

"Guadalcanal fella. They think we hide Malaita folks home to they island. Want cut off Honiara town. No Malaita can go from Honiara."

"Wanna cut off an entire town. Why?"

"So dem fellas kill all Malaita wanna go out."

"Ain't sophisticated political action. What are the Australian soldier-boys doing about it?"

"Dem RAMSI soldiers, gonna fix *olketa*, everything, here."

"Dream on. Captain, we're about 300 feet upriver now. Can we come about and follow the coast again?"

"Dem shoot dere, dat beach."

"So, you say that we are safer here?"

He did not answer. Two sailors, stripped to the waist, came out with a jungle-green parrot on the shorter one's shoulder. The parrot screeched in Pidgin, too fast for my ear.

"I never even noticed this boat's name," I said. "Someday, that kind of tunnel vision may get me killed. Where is her name, anyway? Can't see it from here. What do you call her?"

"C'mon, *mifella*. What you think I call her?"

"Haven't the foggiest."

"The good ship *Laura Nyro*, of course. What you think, *Jumble*?"

"I think that I should have known."

He threw his dark head back and started to sing.

"O! O! My Captain, you are-" he sang.

"I was afraid of that," I said.

Another shot fired from shore.

The parrot blew apart. Blood, gristle and feathers exploded. The sailor dropped. He reached up where the parrot had been. His sailor buddy dodged down near the gunwale.

My palms slapped the deck as I ducked and rolled against the gunwale. It might stop a rifle slug.

"Awwwww!" the sailor screamed.

"You ain't hit!" I shouted. "Cool it!"

"Awwwww! Gaga!"

"Him love long time Gaga he parrot," the Captain said. "Sons of dirty woman!" He yanked his huge pistol from a brown suede holster with the red-and-gray American rebel flag on the flap and fired three shots that hurt my ears.

"Stop shoot, please Jesus, your worship!" he cawed.

"Captain, dem fellas shoot!" the sailor by the gunwale hollered.

"Awwww! Gaga!" the other wailed.

"Damn't think I don't know dem fellas *blong* shoot?" the Captain demanded.

"Your honor," I said. "The question is unclear."

"Less us go open water!" Gaga the Parrot Sailor said. "Dey kill us."

"Fight dem," his buddy said. "Dey kill yo friend Gaga."

"No, no," he said. "No good."

PING!

More shots hit our gunwale.

The Captain cussed and ducked into his cabin.

Ahead of us, on the river, a small skiff about ten feet along put out from shore. A rifle barrel on the skiff bobbed up and fired at us.

I ducked down.

Another skiff moved out from shore.

"They'll move faster than us," I told Gaga the Parrot Sailor. Wiry and young, his face showed stumpy teeth next to bluish tattoos. Tears for Gaga the Parrot ran by the tattoos.

"We go out from ship," he said.

"Yass, man," a third guy said. He had a reddish beard and a bandaged left ear. "Give them ship, *oketa*, everything okay, no problem."

"No!" another bellowed. "We fight!"

"Goddamn right, we fight, please Jesus, your worship," the Captain said. He lugged a metal case about five feet long and two feet wide. It read "Cumberbatch's Finest Vienna Sausage".

"Cap, that much Vienna sausage will make me hurl," I said.

Shots hit. We all ducked again.

He split the case open and yanked out a thick rifle with a leather sling. From old-timey war movies, I recognized it as a Lee-Enfield .303 bolt action rifle. The English soldiers shot it through their colonial wars for the past century. Another sailor grabbed the rifle, knelt by the gunwale and aimed it at the skiffs.

The trigger clicked.

"Stupid dummy, please Jesus," the Captain crowed. "You need bullets. Catch!"

He snorted and slung a magazine at the sailor.

The closer skiff fired a burst of full automatic fire.

The Captain triggered shots back with his dragoon pistol.

He seized another rifle with a cracked wooden stock and a long thin barrel and holstered his pistol.

"Hold on," I said. "That's a .22 you got. Kid's rifle for shooting rats. Shoot that against an assault rifle and you're graveyard dead, Captain. We can't fight these characters with museum pieces like this."

More shots hit. One sailor dropped.

CHAPTER THIRTY FOUR

Gun Power
or
What We Need

The Captain was smoking a cigar as he crouched. Maybe smoking calmed him.

"Modern bullets can destroy your ship, Cap!" I shouted. "They'll get us dead in the water, board us, kill us or chain and starve us in the jungle. Better fight here."

The Captain nodded.

His crew shouted.

"We need more guns!" Captain Mrugank hollered. "Please Jesus, Your Worship!"

I snatched up the .22 rifle from the Captain, checked the load and brought it up to my shoulder.

My shoulder nerves screamed.

Falling downstairs at the airport had damaged Our Hero. I could not bring this gun up to shoot it.

"O, showers of bastards!" I wailed. "I'm aging fast!" Another sailor, looking like a Filipino guy with black bangs and a catfish moustache grabbed the gun from me.

He shot fast without aiming first. He yanked the bolt and fired again. The slugs nipped into the water near the skiff.

On the skiff, a terrorist fired again and hit our deck.

"Ugi kill you all!" he shouted from the skiff. "And Doto, too! Guadalcanal for Ugi!"

The Captain jabbed the cigar from his mouth and took a deep breath. For a second, all lay quiet. His smoker's lungs sounded like a tin bucket kicked down steel stairs.

"Lissen, you sons of economic prostitutes!" he roared over the river at the skiffs. He sounded proud of this professional term. "You know my name! My name is Mrugank! You make trouble for me, and I break you open and use you in dirty places!"

"That's telling them," I said. "Oh, so very precise."

The Captain dealt me a baleful glance.

"Listen, *Laura Nyro* boys!" he roared. "You know law! No guns on boat but for captain. You have gun, shoot now, I am damn't care. Shoot, is okay."

"Truthful?" Gaga the Parrot Sailor asked.

"Captain crazy," his pal, Redbeard, said. "Give us bad food. Too much work, *disfella*."

"Shoot guns, no problem!" the Captain shouted.

His crew of seven clambered below to their bunks.

The heat kept growing. Sweat wetted me.

"Hope they got some fire," I said.

The sailor with tattoos burst onto the deck. He gripped a semi-auto pistol with silver plating and cracked white grips. He sighted down the length of his arm, breathed out and held the pose.

The nearest skiff came through the Mataniku water, sixty feet away. A terrorist stood up in the bow and slammed a magazine into his assault rifle.

"By Jesus, your worship, shoot!" the Captain cawed.

The sailor ignored him, let out a breath and squeezed the trigger. The gun bucked.

The shot hit near the terrorist in the skiff.

"Yaiiiii!" he yelped.

Our sailor aimed and fired again. The terrorist jumped into the water.

"Nice shooting," I said. "You gotta be a hunter. I'm a terrible shot. That joker's still clutching his burp gun. Mataniku water won't help the gun much."

The Filipino sailor was shooting, with fresh slugs clutched in his fingers. His shots missed the skiff.

"Gimme the gun," I said.

"My gun," he said.

"What's your name?" I asked.

He grinned with brown teeth.

"Oscar Gamboa from Samawango."

"Oscar, gimme the gun."

"Sure, boss."

He did.

"Figure that one out," I said.

Now the skiff was about forty feet away.

I locked the rifle against my hip. It hurt my bruises. My hand fired it from the hip, without aiming.

Another sailor, with huge gladiator arms, aimed a revolver that looked like another relic, with rope wrapped around the butt and a pitted rotten finish. He braced it two-handed and fired all six.

Two terrorists jumped from the skiff.

The skiff whirled sideways.

A dugout canoe glided out from shore.

"Go now!" the Captain hollered. "Please, Son of Mary! Get us turned around!"

Shouting scared, they obeyed.

"Dem fella *blong* Ugi!" Redbeard shouted.

"They fake!" Gaga the Parrot Sailor shouted. "Dem fellas Malaita boys! Want blame Ugi!"

"Ugi good fella!"

"Ugi terrorist madman!"

"How you know?"

"No politics, *Laura Nyro!*" the Captain shouted. "We sailors, right? Shut up, work!"

The hunter aimed his gun at the canoe. The trigger clicked.

"No more bullets," I said. "Let's skeedaddle out of here."

"Pardon?"

"Wrong word," I said. "Go. Go, sailor!"

The *Laura Nyro* headed back to Ironbottom Sound.

Our engines revved. Water churned.

"They *tok-tok* politics and stop work," the Captain said. "Then, I damn't trust them. Dey fight each other, we all die."

CHAPTER THIRTY FIVE

Negotiating
or
Laura To the Rescue!

The *Laura Nyro* roared up the Mataniku River, going towards Ironbottom Sound.

Another shot hit, far away.

"That Sound looks safe," I said to Oscar, the Filipino-looking sailor. He squinted at me, like he did not understand. He might be a bit challenged mentally. His dark eyes looked vacant and someone had drawn tiny pen-and-ink swastikas on his denim shirt. It smelled like him.

"Did you draw these?" I asked. "Maybe you don't know what a swastika means. Perhaps you just like the snazzy design."

"Luzon cat-house," he announced. "You give lady the mouth, you no gotta pay. Free."

His own pink tongue darted in and out. He looked like a dumpy lizard in a blue jean swastika shirt.

"Free," he said.

"Concept seems to fascinate you," I said.

The Captain surveyed his boat and turned to my side.

"How you *staap*?" he asked in Pidgin.

"Nobody killed me yet."

"Unhygienic out-of-wedlock!" the Captain snorted. He looked back. Thugs still shot from the skiffs. Their slugs fell short now.

"Ugi try kill us Malaita boys!" Redbeard shouted. "No good!"

"Red," I said. "You look the same as everyone else here. How can anyone tell you're from Malaita?"

"President Doto tell Ugi, protect us!" Tattoos hollered.

"Fetu protect us Malaita!" Redbeard shouted. Cords stood out in his neck. "Fetu good man! Malaita man!"

"Fetu mama smell bad!" Tattoos clamored.

Tattoos shoved Redbeard. Redbeard slapped him with a palm strike VAP!

"Stop damnfool crap!" Oscar shouted. He pushed them apart. "Captain say, work!"

"Been meaning to ask you, Cap," I said. "Where'd you learn your English?"

"Damn't care."

"How long before we reach Marau Island?"

"No Marau."

"Excuse me extremely?"

"Got shot up, hull. Go back Honiara PDQ, Pretty Damn Quick."

This chilled me, even in the morning heat.

"Cap, did I hear you right? I gotta get to Marau."

"*Disfellas* shoot us too much. Bring back Honiara."

"Can't swing that, Cap. Marau Island. That was our deal."

"Shooting. Sons of —"

"Let's leave the family out of this. You work for cash, I know. Two hundred more for getting to Marau Island. American."

"Money no *blong* dis stuff. My boat my stuff. Work."

"Three hundred."

"Boat *blong* my living. Lose him, got nothing."

"You can't stop doing your Marau run just because some fools are popping off guns at you."

We reached Ironbottom Sound and turned left, back to Honiara.

"Cap, this could be real important. Where are the better angels of your nature?"

"Dey mothers."

"What's important to you, Cap? I thought you liked Laura Nyro."

"Huh?"

"I need to hear another of her songs. Which song is your favorite? Play it on your phone for me, please."

"Dis one. 'Lazy Susan'."

"Listen to that voice."

We did.

"It's too bad that nobody on Marau Island will ever hear Laura Nyro," I said.

"How *staap*?"

"Do they know Laura there now?"

"Nao. Cannot."

"Right. And, if I get to Marau, I need your phone to play Laura's songs. To teach them dance. Using her songs. D'you think they will like her songs?"

"Must to be."

"But if we don't get there, nothing happens. No Laura Nyro songs. They will never hear her. But, tell me something. Aren't you the Captain? Like in her songs?"

"I am Captain."

"You say she died young. We can keep her alive. What would she want you to do?"

"Dese crew trash, dey fight Guadalcanal and Malaita want kill, save families. My boat, bloody mess."

"That's just politics, Cap. Noise."

"Bad joss. They fight."

"I can fix that. Gimme another song!"

"'Mercy On Broadway' song?"

"HEY, EVERYBODY!" I bellowed.

"Captain says to dance!"

Some sailors were caulking bullet holes with putty and loud-talking from the adrenaline rush. I felt the same way.

Everyone stopped and stared at me.

Laura Nyro's piano music and voice beat against the engines. Redbeard glared at me.

"Crazy?" Oscar the Filipino asked.

So I grabbed Oscar's wrist and spun him into rock-and-roll position.

"No!" Oscar said.

Oscar looked like the perfect man-child mascot.

The crew loosened up.

Some grinned.

I moved Oscar in the dance. He stopped and then moved.

His tongue darted in and out.

"I'm ignoring you, Oscar. Like a good teacher should. Mother Royster said that being shy wastes everybody's time. Who is brave here?"

Nobody moved.

Tattoos stepped up. I seized his arm and swung him around.

Redbeard grabbed Oscar. They danced.

Others danced.

The Captain climbed the ladder to the cabin. The boat swung around, wake rippling and headed towards Marau Island.

CHAPTER THIRTY SIX

Singing Along
or
I Keep Hoping

"Everybody dance!" I crowed. "Dancing Max is your cabaret huckster!"

"I got good Samawango song!" Oscar shouted. He sang in a drinker's rasp:

O the monkeys have no tails in Samawango/
O the monkeys have no tails in
Samawango/
O the monkeys have no tails/
They were bitten off by whales!/
O the monkeys have no tails in
Samawango!

"Who sails bloody boat, please Jesus, your worship?" the Captain asked.

"You a good dancer?" I asked.

He shouted something in Pidgin, spat over the side and hauled himself into the wheelhouse.

"What's that?" I asked. "That big gray mass thingy over there. Looks like a fat dead whale."

"Shipwreck," Tattoos said. "Some damn ship, Savo Bay battle. Been here after war."

Laura Nyro's voice floated over the engines.

"'Captain Saint Lucifer'," she sang.

"Ugi save Guadalcanal for us!" Tattoos said. Dancing by himself, with arms swinging loose, he bumped into Redbeard.

Both glared at each other.

The Captain steered to the right and leaned down from the wheelhouse door.

"No dance?" the Captain snorted. "Then you go work, by Holy Scripture, yes!"

"I dance!" Tattoos said. He leaped onto one foot, bent the knee and pointed the other toe.

"Very graceful," I said.

"Work, me!" Redbeard said.

He slapped meaty hands on his hip, made an ugly face and swaggered down the stairs to the cot room.

"Seems to be a political divide," I murmured. "Between two warring factions."

"Captain!" Oscar shouted. "Lookout! Wreck!"

Looking forward, I saw a lemon-colored sailboat turned on its side, about a football field ahead of us. Ripples creamed near it. Shapes splashed in the water.

"Captain!" I shouted by reflex.

The dancing stopped.

"Tunny boat!" Tattoos caterwauled.

We slowed.

"Lines!" the Captain roared from the wheelhouse. "Get them out. Fast!"

"Throw lines!" Oscar yelped. "Sharks near here!"

Shaking, I swooped up a coil of line and swung it overhand and tossed one end to a sailor in the water.

"No stop!" Redbeard clamored.

"We gotta!" I said. "Law of the sea. Remember the Birkenhead."

"Whose head?" Oscar asked.

"Classic reference," I said. "Ignore my nonsense. Rescue them."

"You was sailor?" Oscar asked.

"I was baby," I said. "Don't drop the flippin' line."

"Pull her in closer, please Jesus your worship!" the Captain bellowed. "Damn't I know, nobody do sweet Fanny Adams this boat, crew of non entities?"

"Tryna say something, Cap?" I asked.

"Get that one up!" Tattoos shouted. "Looks bloody, thing, that!" Lines pulled a sailor up the side. Gore smeared his face. I leaned into him and sniffed.

Three others were pulling another sailor aboard. He slopped onto the deck. I smelled something.

"Master, master!" my rescued sailor bleated.

He reached backwards into his dripping hair. Metal flashed.

Fear iced my gut.

I moved, too slow.

CHAPTER THIRTY SEVEN

Greed
or
Nothing Changes

The sailor lunged at me.
The razor shone between his fingers.
"UGI RULES!" he screeched.
I ducked.
His hand brushed my throat.
Pain bit me.
I dropped down.
My hand screamed.
"OWWW! Showers of bastards!" I yelped.
He grabbed my hair. My neck bared.
The razor lanced at me.
BAAM!
His hand blew up.
"Goodbye!" I hissed.
I jumped away from him.
"I damn't shoot too quick, hit you!" the Captain shouted from
the wheelhouse. He aimed the Rebel dragoon pistol and fired again.

Orange flame showed.

The gun kicked.

My slasher whipped around sideways. His right pinky showed pink froth.

The razor lay on the deck.

He lunged at me again, missed and grabbed Oscar by the belt.

"Leggo!" Oscar bleated.

He pushed Oscar over the gunwale. Oscar splashed into water ten feet below.

"Don't fight Ugi men!" Tattoos wailed. "He just take boat!"

"Not my boat!" the Captain ripped back. "Not for damn stupid bloody revolution!"

Redbeard spun and kicked out at Tattoos.

Tattoos caught his leg and they hopped back and forth.

Redbeard elbowed him in the gut. Both folded against the gunwale, panting.

"I *tok-tok* you," Redbeard said. He got up. "You just too stupid, revolution, Ethnic Tension."

"*Tok-tok*," Tattoos said. Blood smeared his whiskers. Someone must have hit him.

My slasher tucked his ruined hand into his armpit. Redbeard reached down, scooped up a tin bucket of fish parts floating in water and slammed the bucket into the slasher's face.

My slasher dropped like a wet towel.

Gaga the Parrot Sailor fell backwards, grabbing his thigh.

"Hurts!" he shouted.

Bright red blood spurted from between his fingers.

"Artery!" I shouted. "Lie down! Don't move!"

His eyes glazed and closed.

His blood kept pumping out.

He sprawled against the gunwale and fell overboard.

"Man overboard!" I shouted from training.

In the water, his body spiraled, spewing blood. He went under and vanished.

"Dead, Goddamnit," I said. "Nothing I can do, bleeding out like that."

"Shark fins!" Oscar shouted below.

Two Ugi men swung chains at Redbeard.

The Captain fired a volley. Slugs sparked the chains. One man folded, clutching his bottom. Blood spurted from his back pocket. The other leaped over the side.

"Run, you dock trash!" the Captain snorted. He fired again. "Off my boat!"

"They want boat!" Tattoos belted out. "Pretend be shipwreck."

"Take advantage, my good nature!" the Captain raged. "Help poor wet sailors, by damn! Not no never again!"

"Oscar overboard!" Tattoos cried out.

Limping from my airport catastrophe, I got to the gunwale. Below, Oscar thrashed in the water. A hand reached up from below the surface, took him and pulled him under. Bubbles exploded.

Two more terrorists splashed towards Oscar.

"Them ain't gonna help!" I said. "Oscar!"

Oscar's head broke the surface.

His eyes bugged.

They rolled back in his head.

An arm went around his neck from behind. Oscar choked and spat out water.

"Shoot him!" I bleated at the Captain. "The guy's drowning Oscar."

"Too far!" the Captain said. "Cannot!"

Redbeard seized the rifle, aimed and fired.

BOW!

The rifle blew apart. Splinters flew apart. Redbeard's face opened to blood gashes. His knees buckled.

"Royster to the rescue," I muttered.

Head up, I went over the side.

"Don't!" the Captain bellowed. "Sharks!" The cold water slapped me. My left chest ached. All my energy drained.

"Heart attack, cardiac!" I said.

Oscar thrashed ten feet away.

Three shapes had him.

They punched and choked.

"Dancing Max, way outnumbered," I gasped.

CHAPTER THIRTY EIGHT

Heart Attack
or
Predicting My Future

Three strong youngsters left Oscar. They swarmed around me, splashing water. Salt water stung my cut palm.

"Put you under, *waytii mann!*" one throated.

Cash-poor New Yorkers like me could not swim much in winter. These tropical pirate jokers probably swam every day from birth. Our Hero was in trouble here.

My left chest throbbed.

"AUGG!" I shouted. I reared out of the water. "Doctor! Heart attack!" My hand palmed my chest.

I was faking it. I hoped so. My nerves screamed. Maybe my heart WAS exploding. It was hard to say. One guy swung a dagger at me. I dodged. Water slurped inside my mouth. He slashed again. I spat the water into his eyes. Simple tricks worked best. His slash missed. I forced myself underwater.

METHOD ACTING, I told myself, STANISLAVSKY STYLE. I GOTTA BELIEVE IN MY OWN CHARACTER HAVING AN ATTACK.

Underwater, I saw two legs near me. I put my arm behind the knee, grabbed the foot, locked the leg and pulled him down.

The dagger butt hit my head. I freed my hands, twisted the dagger from his grip and shoved it into his leg. He thrashed. Blood sprayed out. I ground the dagger in deeper.

My lungs burst. I kicked back up and broke the surface, dagger point first.

Like I hoped, the next guy saw the dagger. He reared back, away from it.

"Awww!" his bleeding buddy shouted. He held his leg. Behind them, Oscar fought his attacker.

"Shark!" I cried out. "See shark!"

Maybe they got the message. Blood in the water made things unhealthy here.

My guy stroked away from the dagger. He grabbed the stabbed one by the arm to help him escape me.

"Camaraderie is a wonderful thing," I panted.

Oscar proved it. He got a foot free and kicked it to his attacker's face. The thug ducked down. Oscar turned away, swimming for shore.

For the first time, I noticed the river behind him. This must be the Tenaru. Oscar's attacker lunged at me. I swiped the dagger at his head. He swam away.

"Oscar!" I shouted. "No! Swim for the boat! Not the river!"

Oscar kept going. Maybe he was panicking, like I was. Perhaps he did not hear me. Shaking, I tucked the dagger into the back of my belt and kicked off my shoes. They weighed me down.

His attacker swam after Oscar.

"Boat's safer!" I said. "Got guns there. The ones that don't explode, that is." Oscar kept swimming for shore.

"Now, I gotta chase after the chaser," I said.

My palms smacked the water. Rushing it wasted time. I had to adapt to my crawl stroke.

This was Manhattan's winter and I could not remember the last time that I had swum. Ladies' sunken bathtubs did not count.

Auto fire ripped the water near me.

Someone was shooting from shore.

Behind me, I heard the *Laura Nyro*'s engines rev up. She was approaching me now.

"Captain!" I shouted. "Go upriver! Oscar's heading for shore. Help him out!"

"Yass!" the Captain bellowed from the wheelhouse. He triggered another shot at my stabbed terr.

"Oscar's your crew," I panted. "He's valuable. Worth something. Not like me."

My body fought through the water.

Oscar gained the shore. His blue jean shirt with the swastikas slopped around him.

His thug swam about thirty feet behind him and was closing in fast.

Another gun stuttered from the brush. A huge gunman, bare-chested, wearing Army camouflage shorts and boots sprang from the undergrowth. He clutched a stubby assault rifle to his hip.

"Trouble coming every day," I chanted.

The gunman fired a burst at Oscar. Oscar screamed and dropped on the sand.

The thug behind him splashed out of the water, his back to me. He ran towards Oscar.

I swam crazy, pushed myself ashore, yanked out the dagger and threw it at the gunman, fifty feet away.

That was too much Hollywood. The knife spun and missed him by a yard. He shot at me without aiming. His slugs hit the thug in front of me and spun him around.

"Bloody cock!" the terr shouted at him. "Why you shoot me?"

"Poor training," I said.

More of his pals barefooted out of the jungle.

My gunman cussed something in Pidgin and stepped around a coconut tree to finish me. He aimed.

Nothing happened.

He was out of ammo.

And I was gaining ground on him, barefoot, old, fat and near-sighted in wet clothes.

He looked down at the burp gun. Big mistake. I hit his neck artery with my forearm, all my fat and momentum behind it. Big as he was, he choked. The gun dropped. I snatched it up. It was some kind of metal and plastic deal, with a folding stock. As hard as I could, I slammed the barrel tip into his left eye.

"Owww!" he screamed.

"Here's looking at you, terrorist thug" I said.

CHAPTER THIRTY NINE

Hand To Hand
or
Aging Fast

More terrorist thugs burst out of the jungle.

Nobody had guns. They clutched wooden war clubs.

All I had was an empty burp gun and a pure heart.

One came at me with the club raised. I jabbed the empty gun at him. He jumped back by reflex. "No gun!" he shouted.

"I think you mean bullets," I said.

He slammed his body into me, gripped my hands to cracking bone and twisted the gun away. His hands felt like machinery. Nothing was stopping him. Not me, that was for sure.

"Our Hero," I enunciated, "has now got trouble."

Behind me, something KRUNCHED! The *Laura Nyro* was coming aground on the shoreline's rocks.

"Ayyy, you filth, test-tube offspring!" the Captain gave tongue from the wheelhouse. "Take my boat here on Tenaru! Alligator Alley swamp! We mess you six days Sunday, like Marines mess Japanese, this marsh-land."

"Another historian," I grunted. "Everywhere I look. How do they all find me?" Looking along the river, to the left, acres of mud and marsh oozed in the sunlight.

"They don't call it Alligator Alley for nothing," I said. "No more swimming, all right."

Redbeard, Tattoos and a new sailor, South Asian, bulky and stripped to the waist, brush moustache and huge arms, dropped from the boat to shore. Tattoos hoisted the Captain's Rebel gun.

Redbeard followed.

"Why you here on Alligator Alley?" I asked Redbeard. "Don't you back Ugi?"

"*Laura Nyro* my ship," he said.

"Laura'll be glad to know that, wherever she is," I said. "Soldiers don't fight for a cause. They fight for their buddies." The riverbank looked wet and marshy. I scooped up two rocks, fist-sized and scanned the jungle just as another group ran at us.

Waiting felt hard.

They were just a handshake distance away when I hurled both rocks into the group.

"Getting primitive," I hissed.

My rock smashed a terr's mouth and made him fold up, holding his face in pain. My other rock thudded against a second terr's tattooed bare belly. It slowed the owner down enough for me to duck his club, leap to the side and kick his knee three times barefoot. The last kick knocked him sideways and I rabbit-punched him in the back of the neck until he dropped.

Redbeard jabbed at the nearest thug. The thug made a mistake. He swung a wild haymaker at Redbeard. That let Redbeard step inside the haymaker and jolt him with short sharp strikes to the gut. The thug tried covering his gut by dropping his hands. Redbeard muscled a clumsy right cross that caught him on the nose. It splattered blood and cartilage. The thug took off. Things were getting confusing.

"Kill *waytii mann*!" another thug shouted from inside the jungle.

"Aww, ya mother eats kitty litter," I said. "Be glad I ain't got my weapons system with me. You ever try swimming while you're holding onto a sword cane?"

Some fool fired a shot from the jungle. The slug kicked up sand at our feet.

"Pal," I shouted at the new sailor. "Get back! You need a gun!"

"No gun, boss," he growled back in a deep whiskey voice with an Indian accent. "Got *Kalaripayyatu.*"

"Got what?" I asked. "Is it catching?"

"Dirty," he said.

One thug lunged at him. He punched the thug's left arm, stopped and locked it up. His elbow hit the throat, the man went backwards and a foot swept him down. The sailor lifted his own sneaker and smashed down on the thug's shin. Something cracked.

"Awww!" the thug screamed. He whipped his head sideways, back and forth. My own shins tingled.

"This clown's shin will ache for a while," I said. "Lenox Hill Hospital ain't around the corner, and Guadalcanal's two ambulances are far, far away."

Tattoos fired into the air. A terr hit him with a club to the wrist. He was trying to break the wrist and get the gun. Tattoos leaned back, cursed in Pidgin and kicked the thug under the chin. The thug flew backwards. He folded up, crying. We scanned the hot green jungle for more of them.

The thug still held his wooden war club. I kicked it spinning out of his hand and scooped it up for myself. It was two feet of iron-wood, with a fork at the butt.

"Hey, what's with this stick with a fork in it?" I asked the fighter with no shirt.

He glanced at me holding the club.

"You knock him out, then eat him alive," he said.

"That's motivation to win the fight, all right," I said. "What's your name?"

"Giri," he said. "Why these chaps don't bring their guns here?"

"They're under achievers, Giri. Like the Bible says, if you ain't got the cards, ya can't deal 'em. I didn't notice in the fight but we're already too deep in this Alligator Alley mess. Let's dance back to *Laura Nyro.*"

CHAPTER FORTY

What's Moving?
or
Who Owns It?

"It seems fitting that we have a bit of bovver, what you Yanks call butt-kicking, here at Alligator Alley," Giri said. We were leaping from muddy ground to dry land. Through trees, I could see the Tenaru River but not the *Laura Nyro*. That made me sweat.

"What do you really know about Guadalcanal?" Giri asked.

"World War II stuff, a lot. Today's news, not so much."

"Excellent. Down in my boiler room, I read books all day, all night. So, I need a willing audience. The other sailors just ignore me. Guadalcanal problems began when you Americans brought thousands of Malaitans to Guadalcanal, to finish building that captured Jap airstrip. You needed more workers because the local Guadalcanal folks had scarpered clean away from those bloody Japs."

"And the Malaitans stayed here?" I asked.

"They became the bosses. Trade, government and police service. They make more and live better than Guadalcanal natives."

"Why?"

"Hard to say. You have Black Americans born in your country. I read somewhere that Blacks from the Caribbean or Africa make a lot more money, as a group, than native-born American Blacks do. Why is that?"

"Just guessing," I said. "Maybe better, British-based education, stronger family structure. Controversial stuff to talk about."

"Doto, our Prime Minister, the well-dressed politician, and Ugi agree. Ugi the radical leads these thugs in this swamp. Both Doto and Ugi scream that Guadalcanal should expel all Malaitans. Even those born here. Fetu, the Malaitan, tells his people to fight back."

"There's the boat," I said. "Thank God. Was getting worried."

"Good idea. Look behind you."

Turning, I spied something moving along the swamp, about fifty feet behind us. Sunlight showed the gnarled skin of a croco-gator. He was covering swampy ground, coming our way.

"Alligator Alley, living up to its name, even today," I said. "In Guadalcanal, even the croco-gators push their own history at you. Whether you want it or not."

"Don't antagonize him," Giri said.

"Wouldn't dream of it. How fast can they run?"

"Sufficient."

"And they interrupted your history lecture. What if these gnarled old trees could talk? Look how they are twined around each other. Heavy rainfall does it, I bet."

"You can talk like this, with a *puk-puk* drawing near?"

"I always chatter when I'm scared. Means nothing. Except for dancing, everything on your island scares me."

"Not my island. I come from Kerala in Mother India."

"Think that croco-gator's getting closer to us. There's our shipmates near the river."

Redbeard, Oscar and Tattoos were thrashing through the swampy brush to our left.

"How did we lose sight of them?" I demanded. "And what are they doing over there? Teasing that croco-gator?"

"They moving PDQ, pretty damn quick, now. Suspect that they've seen the croco-gator."

"Don't want to be morbid," I said. "But don't croco-gators travel in packs?"

"Hope not. My engine-room books cover history, politics and economics. Not much about crocodiles, or croco-gators, as you call them."

We neared the boat. Laura Nyro's voice sang from the wheelhouse.

"Where's that croco-gator?" I asked. "Let's get on that damn boat, now."

We were trotting for the boat now. To our right, Redbeard, Oscar and Tattoos broke into a run, splashing Tenaru water.

Something dark lunged from the water and struck Redbeard on the leg.

Oscar shrieked.

"Augh!" Redbeard shouted.

He thrashed down in the water.

"*Puk-puk's* got him!" Giri shouted.

Tattoos kicked the shape. White water exploded. Tattoos grabbed Redbeard by the waist and pulled him up. Redbeard's blue jeans sprayed water. Oscar bent down and put his hand on the croco-gator's head.

"What's Oscar doing?" I asked. "Looks like he's trying to pet that monster. Either crazy or real brave."

Far away, I saw Oscar stick his tongue out at the croco-gator.

They ran towards the ship.

Redbeard ran bare below the waist.

The croco-gator held his blue jeans in his jaw. The blue jeans seemed to choke the gator. He kept trying to bite through the material.

"Saw those blue jeans up close awhile ago," I said. "No showers on the boat. Lot of oil, fish chum and dirt in Redbeard's blue jeans. Hope the gator don't get poisoned by them."

"What?"

"Maybe I can ask the gator that personally," I said. My voice choked. Running was stealing my breath. "'cause he's coming this way."

The croco-gator was chasing us now, blue jeans still in his jaws. They trailed behind him in the water. Swimming, he moved faster.

Laura Nyro kept singing.

River tides pushed our boat twenty feet from shore.

All of us splashed into the water.

Shapes showed in the water.

"*Puk-puks*!" Giri said. "Coming at us!

CHAPTER FORTY ONE

Local Stuff
or
Why They Got Teeth

The Captain threw a line off the stern for us.

The line splashed in the water. A gator nipped at it.

"Grabbing that line might prove risky," I hissed out. "Look at those croco-gators blocking us from the boat."

"Don't move anything," Giri said. He stayed still.

"Are you kidding?" I asked. "I ain't waiting."

Carrying my bruises as fast as possible, I dashed across the water towards the boat. Oscar, Tattoos and Bare Redbeard froze in the water.

The Captain tossed another line. The gator was chewing on the first line.

Croco-gators swam at me.

In mid-air, I jumped, caught the line and swung towards the boat like a fat-bellied Tarzan. My bare feet slammed against the hull. I got one foot against the hull, pushed off and tried getting into the boat.

Five feet below my groin, gator jaws opened obscene. He snapped upwards from the water, brushing my foot.

My chest and ribs slammed across the stern and I tumbled into the boat.

"How damned you can do that jump?" the Captain asked.

"Croco-gators," I wheezed. "They inspired me."

"Huh?"

"Remembered reading somewhere, strongest bite on the planet. That's inspirational, Captain."

"You should wait," he said. "Watch what I do."

He stepped up the step-ladder back to the cockpit and started the engines. Then he gunned them louder.

"Look, the croco-gators!" he cawed. "They swimming away!"

"Why?"

"They damn't like the noise! You should wait for Captain. You risk your life for nothing!"

"Again?"

Oscar, Redbeard, Tattoos and Giri waded through the water and hoisted themselves onto the boat by climbing up the lines. They looked used to it. Handling heavy lines gave them power in the hands and arms.

Exhausted, I stripped off my sweaty shirt and sank down on the deck. Heat grew.

"How you get them marks, bruises?" Redbeard asked, checking his bare bottom for bite marks. He pointed to my purple and red and black marks where I had fallen down the airline ladder. "Did goddamn gator do that you?"

"Not unless he works part-time at Henderson Field," I said.

"You all hurt, man," he said in his high-pitched lilt of a voice, like most of the locals.

"Maybe so. But I'm still wearing my pants. Why don't you cover up your back porch? Some of these sailors look kinda raunchy. Oscar, for example. Someone might try teaching you a new way."

"Look to you self, man," Redbeard said. He thumped his chest, covered by an immaculate red T-shirt with the reggae singer Bob Marley stamped on it. Many other Melanesians wore that same shirt. It was a long stretch of memory since Bob Marley had died 14,000 miles and almost forty years ago. The Guadalcanal locals saw common ground with him and wore his T-shirts like flags.

"That all damn finish now, battle of Tenaru River and Alligator Alley," the Captain hooted. "No unsavory parentage-type Ugi stop the *Laura Nyro*. We go to Marau Island."

That made me snap to.

"For real, Captain?" I asked.

"You teach dance-dance with Laura Nyro music?"

Plain talk seemed called for.

"I promise."

"Then, we go. All ahead, half!"

"He really going?" Oscar asked.

"You bet your tongue," I said. "That's great, Cap. I'm with you. I gotta find Rua."

"Who?" the Captain asked.

For a moment, I weighed telling him. Guadalcanal locals lived by gossip. They shunned cell phones and the Internet, even if they had them available. Nobody held cell phones in my view.

Not yet, I decided. Telling him could simmer a bit.

"We need more mysteries in our lives," I said.

LIKE HELL, I thought.

"Need a good tucker and kip," Giri said. "After changing clothes."

"If you mean food and sleep, you're talking to the right man. Right now, I could breast-stroke through a sewer and sleep and not wake up until Christmas."

"Extra clothes, you take here," the Captain said. "Boat clothes, we keep on boat."

"And I'm sure they've got an interesting history," I said.

"You always wisecracking about Guadalcanal stuff," Giri said. "This is not my land but that bothers me. Must figure that Guadalcanal and all the Solomons, damn poor spots. Nobody got money, never. Nobody famous ever came from this part of the Pacific. Guadalcanal is so far away from everything. It is the least visited place in the world."

"Less than the South Pole?"

"People go to the South Pole for a culture event and make a big splash about it. Nobody does that here. Malaria, the climate and the Ethnic Tension murders keep tourists away. Would you bring your kids to somewhere on holiday where they get malaria? Your Marines learned that malaria never goes away. What do you know about the Battle of Guadalcanal?"

CHAPTER FORTY TWO

Dreaming Again
or
Marine Boot

Dressed in the stiff salty clothes held in common by the *Laura Nyro*, I chawed down some oily tasting fish and a greenish rice mixed with sweet peas and hunted for a berth below deck.

Humid air dried my skin and bruises and the rhythm hum of engines rocked me to sleep. Giri's talk about Guadalcanal's battle in 1942 gnawed at my brain. Again, I was dreaming. The dream was sharp-edged and very real. This is what I remembered later, from my dream.

•

Guadalcanal
August 8, 1942

"Japs start digging out this airstrip," Corporal Tex said.

He always had the inside dope, the straight scuttlebutt, from the top. His broke nose against watery no-color eyes wagged whenever he whispered secrets. He looked like someone you would forget two minutes after seeing him. Like Marines sometimes did, we were just shooting the breeze and throwing our new K-Bar knives into a coconut tree. Two other leathernecks practiced judo chops with their hands against a bigger tree.

"Bare-ass naked natives see this, tell some Aussie planter who tells our Navy jokers. Big brass in Washington know nuttin' bout Guadalcanal. Island so far-off, it got lost and not found again, hundred years. Admirals got a crummy old map and a Jack London story bout here. That's it. They figger, amphib land us here, see what gives."

"Like always, us Marines are what gives," I said. I was trying to ape the old-timers, the regulars. So I wisecracked. Nobody smiled. The air hung. I started sweating through my greens.

One bald Marine throwing the knife stopped and stared at me. The big K-Bar blade gleamed.

"You ain't a Marine yet, junior," another Marine said. They called him Yardbird. "You Parris Island boot. Know nothin', worth the same, prolly git ya buddies dead."

My breath sucked in.

Nobody spoke for me. Their slim tough faces clenched.

"Want me to go?" I asked. My voice broke on the last word. In my battle greens, I half rose up.

"Aww, siddown, boot," some Marine said. The shadow from a coconut tree trunk blacked him out. A reddish glow showed him smoking a butt. "Corps might pipeline us someone even dumber."

"Hard to imagine," Corporal Tex said. "So, the old man, General Vandergrift, sends our butts over here, see if the Japs really got Coke-bottle specs, they can't see to shoot."

"So far, it's good duty," another Marine said. He sported premature white hair in a crew cut and a button nose. "Got their grub, they booze, lousy smokes, they turned tail like a turpentined dog and prolly loading inna transport, get outa here."

"Our swabbies ferrying our stuff ashore right now," Corporal Tex said. "Steaks, hardtack, beans and java. Ammo for Tommy guns. Grenades. Navy servicing Marines. Like they should. Gonna look like garrison in the Philippines. We can sack out, sleep like rocks."

"Figure that way?" Yardbird said. "Here comes Washing Machine Charley. Tryna wreck our sack-time, with his gacked-up motor."

The Washing Machine Charley, a Jap scout plane, bumbled overhead, red lights winking.

"Any officers around?" Yardbird asked.

"Nope. Big powwow, Officers' Country."

"Let's show Charley the Marines have come to call," Corporal Tex said. "Royster, stand fast. Don't waste your ammo."

Tex raised his Tommy gun at Wa;shing Machine Charley three hundred feet up. The others hoisted their Springfields and aimed.

"HOORAH!"

Everyone fired except me.

Guns kicked. Shells from the Tommy sprinkled golden in the gloom.

"That 30-06 round will go through Charley's canopy," Corporal Tex said. "Even from here. Show that to his pan-faced buddies. Tell 'em Marines defend their sack-time."

"Yeah," Yardbird said. He worked the bolt of his Springfield.

"Royster, get you another weapon in the morning," Corporal Tex. "Sign for it, then. Can't have you running around without one."

"Royster's okay," Yardbird said. "Signed up, didn't he?"

That floored me. Yardbird was giving me an okay.

"Good kid, yeah," the knife man said.

"I getya," the white-haired Marine grunted.

For no reason, they were changing their minds about me. It was a mystery.

My smile stretched so hard that it hurt my jaw. Then I covered it up so nobody could see. "Smoking lamp is out!" someone called.

Smiling, I slept.

KARRUMPH!

Shrapnel hit. I rolled over, grabbing the shotgun.

Out on the water, a plane's white lights overhead caught a US ship.

"Jap float plane!" someone hollered. "Setting our swabbies up!"

"Go port!" Yardbird shouted. "Left, ya fathead skipper!"

But our ship sailed straight.

"Turn!" someone hollered.

Our ship blew apart. White tracers shot everywhere. Figures fell overboard. I screamed from shock.

CHAPTER FORTY THREE

Dream Goes On
or
Scared Me

My dream continues.

•

More boat guns fired.

My body did not want to leave the Marine Corps rubberized jungle poncho. The old-timers said that it could protect us against shrapnel. One hand held my sawed-off and the other the cowboy Peacemaker six-shooter.

"Boot!" Corporal Tex snapped. "Skipper says those Japs can throw a 270 pound shell about 12 miles. They train those guns on us, your li'l popgun there won't do much."

"Jap Float-Plane!" Yardbird hollered. "Lighting our boys up!"

Different planes overhead dropped fat wavy white lights over the ships.

Under the light, a gray US cruiser turned about.

"No!" Yardbird. "Don't give them no big target!"

He sounded hopeless.

Streaks of fire blew from the Jap ship. Shells slammed into the US ship.

It bucked and broke apart like a toy. The flares still hung overhead.

"We'll hit 'em back twice as hard," I said. "We gotta. Can't lose this war."

"Yes, we can, youngster," Yardbird snapped. "Think this is Hollywood with a happy ending alla time? Manchuria lost, the Philippines lost. So did Malaysia, Indonesia and China's losing now. Nothing's stopped these Japs so far."

Another ship exploded, farther out. Tracers arced and fell into the water.

"We sure ain't stopping them tonight," Corporal Tex said. "Lookit them rounds bursting."

"Just like fireworks back home," I said.

"See those swabbies gotta dive deep," Yardbird muttered.

"Why?" I asked.

"Or else, they fry when the engine oil escapes and fires up that ocean. It gets to be a real mess. Anyone afloat is cooked all crisp."

"Lookit leaves moving here," Yardbird said. "Shock waves, concussion from them Navy guns, I bet."

"That far away?" I asked.

"Shock waves travel, boot. Like down in Tacloban, the Philippines."

"We getting murdered out there," Corporal Tex said. "Let's grab the company commander, see what he wants done. You stay here, Royster. Keep watch, huh?"

"Nahhh," I said, without thinking.

"Why the hell not? Ya scared to be alone or something? Well, suck it up, buttercup. Be right back."

They left.

More white gun-lights ripped the night out on the water. Our cruiser burned, going in crippled sick circles. Sounds of men crying out carried across the inky waves.

Nobody was near me.

Like always, the China Marines, the old-timers, grouped together about fifty feet away and watched the sea battle together. They drew near the beach. They acted like coming closer to the fighting would help our side. More leaves rustled.

The wind smelled foul.

Something moved on my left.

I ducked down and fired.

The sawed-off kicked up. It tore out of my grip.

"Yaaaoow!" I hollered.

My body whipped around to find the shotgun, in the brush behind me. Whoever it was might still be out there.

"What's up, boot?" Corporal Tex yelped. His Tommy gun snout roved across the jungle. "You see the Japs?"

"Uh," I said.

"You drop your weapon, accidental?"

"The kick," I said. "Not used to it."

"See what?" Yardbird shouted.

"Jap," I said. "Right there."

I pointed the empty sawed-off. Then I saw the skin of the tree ripped up. There was no Jap there. The tree branch had moved in the offshore breeze and I had panicked and shot without looking. Without making sure of my target.

"Ya sure?" another Marine asked. He pointed his Springfield with the strong leather sling around his left arm for a steady shot.

My face burned. I could not tell the truth.

"Lauten," Corporal Tex said. "Take Czarsky and check for infiltrators. Japs shouldn't be in this close to us."

"Ya don't gotta —" I said.

"Why not?" Corporal Tex snapped. "Ya saw them, didn't ya?"

There it was again.

"Sure, I saw them," I said. Even to me, I sounded fake.

"'cause no reason, risk their butts if you're just seeing things."

"Saw him," I repeated.

"'kay, then. Move out, clowns."

"If you're tryna protect me, you're screwing up," I said. "I'm all alone again."

Nobody heard me.

"Old Corps," I muttered. "China Marines. Tough as gun leather, all right, but not deep thinkers."

Just like before, I was isolated.

To keep up my spirits and guts, I sang under my breath:

My granddaddy was a China Marine.

Spent his life just a-wearing green.
Ate his steaks three inches thick,
Cleaned his teeth with a swagger stick!
The buckshot ripples on the tree trunk fascinated me so I went up to touch them.

"To make it look good , there should be some Jap blood on it," I said. "Yeah, right quick!"

Something moved.

I whipped my bayonet out and slashed.

CHAPTER FORTY FOUR

**Still Dreaming
or
The War Goes On**

My Dream Continues

●

Something scared me. But my bayonet just cut air. My slash caught my own left hand with the tip of the bayonet.

"Owww!" I mewed. "Damn!"

I was already shedding blood Somewhere In the South Pacific but it was my blood. The bayonet slid back into my belt scabbard.

Taking the blood from my own hand, I smeared it on the buckshot marks along the tree trunk.

"Take that, Jap night-fighter," I said aloud. "Next time's for real."

"No more, *mifella*" a voice said. "You shoot me."

I dropped flat and my shotgun went flying.

"What's that?" I shouted.

"Missionary boy," the man's voice said. "How you *staap*?"

"What you doing here, near our lines?"

"Auw?"

"Stealing, right? Like all you characters."

I yanked the cowboy pistol from my musette bag and pointed it at the voice.

"Get out here, hands up!" I shouted. "We're supposed to shoot anyone approaching our lines."

A small Black man, no more than five feet six inches, stepped towards me. He held my shotgun, open in his left hand, with empty barrels showing in the glow of burning ships.

Rushing to lie, I had forgotten to re-load my shotgun. The extra shells rattled in my musette bag.

"Why you shoot me?" he said.

"Orders, Mac."

"Look here," he said.

He lifted a knotted arm oozing blood near the elbow. Layers of skin showed in the half-light from burning ships. Bumps from the buckshot reminded me of the tree.

"Japanese come quick, you fellas asleep, not see and lose boat."

"You can't tell yet."

"Look."

We scanned the starburst water, with purple and red and white bursts as ship magazines exploded. Fuel tanks ruptured. Planes zig-zagged overhead. Jungle birds cawed.

"Gimme the weapon, clown," I said. Marine jargon covered my feeling dumb.

"Take it. Me don't like guns. Now guns make big trouble everything, *garem*."

"You got that right, joker."

"Light come from Japanese, show you boats okay, no problem," he said. "Big bang."

I could not stop watching. He was right. We were losing ships fast. Another one blew apart, swirling in the water.

More flares lit the scene.

Burnt oil smell blew into my nose.

Washing Machine Charley coughed overhead.

My joker was about forty, with a worker's body covered by just a green cloth around the hips and rubber sandals. His bare chest muscles and twists of flesh heaved. Maybe I was scaring him.

A full beard jutted out from teeth reddish stained by betel nut juice.

"You frighted, then shoot me," he said.

"Maybe I finish the job now. Shut you up for keeps. Nobody know. Or care."

"Gun got nothing."

"You're right, Tarzan. Embarrassing. Just wait. Now that's all fixed. Two more slugs for your butt."

"Japs treat us good better than English Johnnies do," he said. "Japs say 'Asia for Asiatics'. No *moa* White Johnnies, be big boss man. You know what we fella call them Dutch Johnnies?"

"Something vicious, I bet."

"Call them 'cheese-heads'."

"What's that talk?" a new voice asked. "Who there?"

The voice was loud and close and Marine.

Fear corkscrewed me tight.

Marines would shoot him.

Or take him captive and hear how I had panicked and shot him. One deal seemed worse than the other.

"Here!" I hissed, grabbing my poncho. "Flatten!"

He dropped and I threw my poncho over him. He budged. I kicked him to shut him up.

Yardbird and two Marines stepped out of the jungle.

"Talking to yourself, boot?" Yardbird asked. "You gone Asiatic?"

"Combat fatigue?" another snickered. Squat and dark, he looked suspicious of everything, including me and the poncho next to me. "'cept the boot ain't seen no combat yet."

"Seeing it now," the other Marine said. He looked like his own Springfield rifle, lean and craggy and serviceable, ready to kill. His head bobbed under the old-fashioned flattish helmet, from the 1918 war. "Japs clobbering our swabbies out there."

"Enough skylarking," Yardbird said. "Sarge wants us on the perimeter. This still a forward area. Japs can infiltrate."

"Boot, police up your poncho," the dark one said. "Crud crawlers get into it."

They left. Their Springfields probed the dark.

Out to sea, more ships exploded.

"I should have given you over to them as a thief," I said. He stayed flat as I lifted the poncho. His arm bled more.

"Japanese treat us like men. We help Japanese get us our free."

"Stow it, clown. Get off my ear with that. What's your name, anyway?"

"Ugi."

CHAPTER FORTY FIVE

Worse Than Pearl Harbor
or
What Can I Do?

My dream continues.

●

Out on the moving mica-chip water, ships kept shooting and exploding.

"Ha! Ha!" a voice came across a PA system in perfect English. "You keep missing us! You know that we have better radar and better gunners. Surrender and get back to your wives and children in peace."

"Lousy Japs," I echoed my rifle squad and just about everyone else.

"Wanna win, must get friends with islands *wantoks*," Ugi said. "Or else, you another boss *waytii mann*. And nobody gonna help you."

"Can't trust Japs, pal."

"Black *wantoks* can't trust nobody."

"Why not? I didn't shoot ya, did I? Jeez, lookit those boats burn."

"American don't care these Pacific. Why you fight? Let Yellow and Black people hold islands. Go back American."

A destroyer cut through the battle water. Another Jap flare lit up the scene. A US flag showed on the destroyer's prow. The forward gun fired.

Two hundred yards ahead, the shell hit a ship and exploded. The flare showed a Jap cruiser, reeling from the shot.

The destroyer fired three more hits that spun the cruiser around.

"That's the stuff!" I shouted. "Clobber them!"

The destroyer closed in.

The Jap turned broadside.

"Kill him!" I shouted.

"Blast him back to Tokyo!" another Marine bellowed, far to my left.

"Drop the yellow-bellies!" a New England accent added.

WHAM!

The destroyer exploded. Our ship went flying into pieces.

"Submarine!" somebody shouted. "Torpedo took them out!"

"What's those flames moving out there?" someone asked.

"That's men caught fire," Yardbird said. "Tryna swim away from the ship."

"Can hear 'em screaming," Corporal Tex. "Count four of our cruisers out there on fire."

"And the Japs?"

"Nothing much. None of them on fire."

We watched the slaughter all night. Dawn broke. The Jap ships left. Our ships burned.

My eyes stayed on the ships.

Ugi twisted the shotgun and grabbed it out of my hand before I could move. He ran towards the bush. His feet pumped.

"Hey!" I shouted. "Can't do that!"

My hand dug in the musette bag and came up with the cowboy gun. By reflex, I pointed it at Ugi.

Out to sea, another ship exploded.

My gun sights centered on Ugi's back. Squeezing the trigger would kill him. I froze. I could not shoot him.

Gun flashes lit up everything. The others saw Ugi running.

"Sneak thief!"

"Infiltrator!"

Corporal Tex opened up with his Tommy gun. The gun went BUDDA BUDDA BUDDA!

Slugs tore Ugi up and flopped him down. He tumbled and lay flat.

"Dead as a mackerel," Corporal Tex said. He prodded him with a boot.

"He stole somebody's gun," Captain Anhalt said, coming up with his .45 out. "Anybody ever seen this weapon before?"

"Yessir," I said.

"Royster, shut up," Corporal Tex said. "That weapon's not Marine Corps issue. Nobody's authorized to carry it. Get brig time for it. Cap, Royster's just shook up. First action, ya know. Dead joker prol'ly stole the gun from some Brit plantation here. What's with our ships, sir? That's real stuff."

The Captain holstered. He hesitated, looking at us. His hands shook. That scared me. The Captain had fought in France, Haiti and Nicaragua, wounded twice, with a Silver Star medal.

"Got the straight dope, Tex. We lost three cruisers, more than a thousand sailors," the Captain said. Now he looked older than before, sharp lines in the sagging bulldog face with white stubble. "Intel just gave me the word. Worse than Pearl Harbor last year. Navy's worst defeat. We got supplies and ammo for ten days. After that, we starve. Japs use us for bayonet practice."

Shaking, I hid back under my poncho. It felt safe there.

BUDDA BUDDA! gun noise pounded in my head.

Washing Machine Charley flew overhead.

Shrapnel hit my poncho.

BUDDA BUDDA!

More nights passed.

The Japs were coming.

I kept weeping.

CHAPTER FORTY SIX

No More Dream
or
I Ain't Dead Yet.

My dream ended.

The *Laura Nyro* kept chugging under my bruises.

My shirt collar felt sweaty. My war dream had felt very real.

"Surrounded by history nuts here," I grumbled to Redbeard. He was squatting on his heels in the cabin, chewing betel nut and spitting into a tin tuna can.

"All you characters gassing about the war, goes into my subconscious."

Redbeard spat out more betel nut juice.

"It's only here on Guadalcanal that I suffer these weird war dreams," I went on. "Back in Manhattan, I just have ordinary dreams with everyday material. Blonde actresses breaking down my apartment door to bed me, free Maker's Mark Bourbon, pistachio ice-cream. Normal stuff. It's this exotic background with the Hollywood jungle setting that does it to me. I may never straighten out again and get like the other boys."

Redbeard scratched himself intimately.

The *Laura Nyro* slowed.

My bruises from the airport fall ached more now. Maybe I had gained some new hurts fussing at Alligator Alley. My bones and skin and cartilage throbbed.

The Captain forwarded his Laura Nyro files to my phone and I learned everything about her.

We had gone inland from the coast and were coming across a wide flat bay to an island.

"That's Marau Island?" I asked Redbeard.

He nodded.

Up close, I saw that his beard covered a network of tribal scars on both cheeks. Maybe his own Melanesian culture had required the scars. There was so much that I did not know about these islands and their people. It made me feel small and alone, trying to find Rua in this strange world.

Marau Island looked oblong to me, with a wide sandy beach about sixty feet from the jungle. Low waves broke over grey rocks and reminded me of Rockaway Beach back home in New York. It looked like you could walk around it in about two hours, staying on the sand. Avoiding the jungle seemed like a good idea. Because some shots from shore still cracked towards our boat.

"I'm almost getting used to these snipers winging slugs at us," I told him. "You can get used to anything. Like sleeping when Washing Machine Charley cranks his engines overhead."

"Who?"

"Never mind. Local historical figure. I know that this boat is a big easy target for bored *wantoks* who aren't working. But why does Ugi and his ilk keep shooting at us?"

"Ugi want to keep *blong* Malaita *wantoks* in Honiara."

"Why?"

"Show he power. Kill them, maybe."

"That's a lot of people."

"And Ugi gun at our boat, so he stop business, copra, tunny fish. Dem soldiers *blong* Australian, *olketa*, can do nuttin', cannot stop Ugi. That what Guadalcanal got, make cash."

"I read about gold here. Does Ugi try stopping the gold mines?"

"Gold mines closed for years. No *moa*. We, Pacific Blacks, got nothing."

"It just hit me. You could be right. You got very little here."

"Nuttin'."

"No industry, Ethnic Tension, miles from everywhere, no tourists hungering to get the kids infected lifetime with malaria. Aussie troops just showing the flag, colonial politics. And the only ones who ever heard of you are World War Two history buffs."

Our boat slowed. Waves rippled out. We were drawing near a wide concrete pier jutting out from the shore. A wide Black man with a blond streak growing whitish in his hair stood on the pier. Rows of what looked like ivory hung on his chest. He wore just a loincloth around his hips and nothing else. Gold and silver bracelets winked on his wrists and arms. He was thick and stout-built, not fat, and moved with gravity.

"Big-Man Sako," the Captain shouted from the wheelhouse.

"*Kastom* say greet you," the Black man said. "How you *staap*?"

"*Mi hapi foa lookim yiu moa*," the Captain said in Pidgin. "*Got dis fela* Ugi *hurt boat blong mi tumas*."

"UGI *blong kolsap*," the Black man said.

"Sailor," I said. "What does '*kolsap*' mean?"

"'Close by' *blong disfela*."

"Load up PDQ," the Black man.

"'PDQ' means 'Pretty Damn Quick,'" I said. "That sounds like the language of business Pidgin."

"Oscar, make fast dem lines, please Jesus your worship, or I will have to intercourse some inanimate object," the Captain said.

"Wish I'd said that," I said. "Oscar, lemme help you."

"You passenger!" the Captain hollered at me.

"Cap, lemme tell you about my dream."

"Just stand down. My crew obey me."

Laura Nyro kept singing about time and love. The Black man swayed a bit to her music. Melanesians were a dancing people, after all.

Something crawled on my wrist.

A fat spider sprawled there. I tried shaking it off. It held on.

"Funnel-spider!" Oscar shouted.

"Poison!"

CHAPTER FORTY SEVEN

Squashing Danger
or
Saved By the Dump

I screeched, "AAYYY-AH!"
So did everyone else.
"Will kill you!" Tattoos shouted.
Sailor training kicked in.
I jumped overboard.
Water would fix it. I reached out.
I hit concrete.
My arm felt broken.
My head smacked backwards.
"What you do?" the Captain roared.
"Jumped," I said. "Wrong side of the boat."
I was sprawled on the dock. My leap was okay. It was just the wrong side.
"Where spider?" Oscar asked. "That funnel-spider, there. Poisonous!"
"Look," I said. The spider lay flat, squashed, dead and oozing something pink and ugly on my wrist. The wrist felt broken.
"How you kill the spider?"

"My wrist got caught under my bottom. Landing on the dock did the rest."

"So you mash spider with your own ass," Oscar said. "Thinking quick. Lookit your arm. Make sure he not bite you."

"If he bite you, we just shoot you," Tattoos said. "Do you big favor. That bite make you go crazy, suffer, cry for days. Better dead."

"Easy for you to say," I said.

"Nobody dies from a funnel-spider bite," the Black man said. "At least, not this week."

It took me a second to realize that his speech was clear and precise, without Pidgin or slurring. He stood out among the others and I had gotten used to the Guadalcanal speech rhythms of everyone else.

Wanting to pump him up and get him on my side, I tried getting up with all the dignity of a senior citizen who had just squashed a spider with his lower forty.

"Captain, will you please present me?" I asked.

The Captain rose to the occasion. His sailors straightened up and stopped talking.

"This is Big-Man Sako," the Captain said. "He rules Marau Island. Please your worship, he make all big decision, programs, spreadsheets here –"

I wondered what spreadsheets had to do with running the island.

"– marry couples, *tok-tok* arguments and punish bad ones. This Marau Island, sacred ground, the *kastom* here. Nobody buy or corrupt it."

"Hopefully, not," Big-Man Sako said. He smiled. His arm looked as large as my leg and active muscles pulsed there whenever he moved. His massive head turned on a wide neck. "But Ugi wishes to take this island and kill us or force us off."

"Why, Big-Man?" I asked.

"To show his power."

"Like how he kidnaps tourists?" I asked, fishing for a word about Rua.

"Ugi does not kidnap," Big-Man Sako said. "Kidnapping is a hated crime everywhere. It violates our Solomons *kastom*. No, Ugi is a politician. He seduces. He is now cavorting with a young White female, around our island. They appear to be lovers."

That snapped my head up, forgetting all about the spider, the gunshots and my bruises.

"Who gave you this?" I asked.

Big-Man Sako regarded me.

"Your tone," he said.

He made me feel like a spanked schoolboy.

"Please accept my apology, Big-Man Sako," I said. "Sorry for my tone."

"Accepted. I saw them myself, swimming and embracing. She looked young and to those without much of life, a radical idealist may seem like a hero. As we age, we gain more perspective."

"Not me."

Part of me wanted to say that the young White woman might be my daughter, Rua. That might get these traditional types to help me more. She could have fallen for Ugi. A younger version of Diana, the sex risk-taker and sensualist, would have taken Ugi as a lover. Again, my body ached for Diana.

"Ugi has a large group of gunmen and thugs," Big-Man Sako went on. "He wants us, all of us 189 *wantoks,* here, to flee in terror from his guns. He calls himself an atheist. We are Animists here, believing that all things have life. And Marau is the center of life on Guadalcanal, as our fathers taught us."

"Boat coming!" Oscar shouted. "Never seen it before."

"That's Ugi," Big-Man Sako said. "With his gun." He might have been discussing the weather.

Ugi, as I remembered him, piloted a blue speedboat and crested on white water a hundred yards away. The boat swerved closer.

One-handed, he lifted something straight from the boat. Orange fire spurted from it.

"Down!" I shouted. Everyone flattened.

"We know dat," Oscar said.

My NYPD reflexes took over.

"Shots fired!" I bellowed, from habit.

They looked at me.

"Probably know that, too," I muttered.

Feeling dumb, I used the traditional NYPD way of covering up stupidity. I fixed my face into the look of a long suffering and hot-tempered tough veteran.

A woman's red head bobbed next to Ugi in the boat.

The Captain drew and fired his gun at Ugi.

"DON'T!" I shouted. "That's my daughter!"

CHAPTER FORTY EIGHT

Daddy Talk
or
I Come Clean

Everyone stared at me.

Ugi's boat came closer.

"You say she is your daughter?" Redbeard said. "How you know?"

"Her mother showed me pictures," I said. "Sent me some by email. Her high school prom pictures on Skype."

"Modern marriage," Big-Man Saku said in his bookish tones. "Never shall I comprehend."

"Me, neither," I said.

"Cannot shoot the son of failed Artificial Insemination," the Captain said. "I might hit your daughter by mistake, boat bouncing like that."

"Please, nobody shoot," I said. "Ugi is not trying to kill us. He is just announcing the revolution again."

"We don't shoot, he get more brave," Oscar said.

"I come to tell you Malaitans on Marau Island!" Ugi shouted. "Leave the island today. Go back to Malaita where you belong. This Marau Island is in Guadalcanal, not Malaita. You are stealing our land. Again."

"We Malaitans have been here for on the island for many years," Big-Man Saku said. "Nobody called us thieves before. And Guadalcanal people never wanted to live here, without electricity or running water. So, only Malaitans here. Why does he do this now?"

"Needs an issue for the voters," I said. "So he creates the issue. We have politicians back home who do the same thing."

Out on the water, Ugi drove the boat closer to us. It looked like he was daring us to shoot.

"Leave today, in peace!" he shouted. "We can stop your fresh water and watch your children die of thirst."

He whipped the boat around so sharply that he looked like he was trying to capsize it.

He fled back west along the coast waters, towards Honiara.

We looked at each other.

"Big-Man Saku, can he really stop your water supply?" I asked.

"If no rain comes, yes. The Captain brings us fresh water every week. We have no fresh water streams on Marau. Before, in emergencies, we caught rainwater in tins and survived that way."

"And I'm feeling thirsty already," I said.

"Stop making wisecrack jokes, New Yorker," the Captain said.

"The name is Max. And what you're asking is impossible for any real New Yorker."

"I going radio those Aussie troops, this threat," the Captain said.

"You know what they will tell us," Big-Man Saku said. "Like before. They say, leave Marau. They say they cannot spare soldiers to defend 189 fools like us on 126 acres of worthless island."

"Why are the Australians here?" I asked. "Guadalcanal is independent."

"They call themselves RAMSI," the Big-Man Saku said. "Regional Australian Military Stability Infantry. They are supposed to be operating under a United Nations mandate to stop the Ethnic Tension here."

"And doing a bang-up job of it," I said.

"There you go again," Big-Man said.

"Sorry," I said.

"Ugi is an unusual type," the Chief said. "He belongs to the Divine Light Of Being religion on Guadalcanal. Like Christians, they believe in heaven and hell. And, if they lie, they go to hell. Do most Christians believe that now?"

"Not hardly," I said. "Especially politicians."

"But Ugi does. He cannot lie."

"He lied when he said that he had proof that you Malaitans want to destroy Guadalcanal from within," I said. "Heard him myself."

"He didn't lie. I'm sure that he has what he calls proof. But the rest of us would call it gossip."

"Just like back home," I said. "In Gracie Mansion."

"I knew Ugi's family," Redbeard said. "Always very serious boy."

"What's his religion called, where he can't lie and must keep his word?" I asked.

"Divine Light of Being. Is nutty, yeah?"

"Maybe not," I said. "They got any women in that religion? Maybe it's about time I got married again."

"If that is your daughter embracing Ugi, then it seems that you have failed as a father," Big-Man Saku said. "You should not attempt it again."

"Big-Man, we're kind of rushing to load the Laura Nyro now," I said. "I don't have time to explain today's modern divorce cycle to you."

"Yank, show some respect," the Captain said. "We are his guests here."

"Excuse me, Big-Man," I said. "Seeing my daughter shook me bad. After all these years, I'm still in love with her mother."

It felt like the truth. This was a great place to discover it.

"Captain, can your boat get back to Honiara?" I asked.

"Maybe. If Ugi be careless. Or he let us pass."

"Are any other boats coming from Honiara?"

"Why you want to know this?"

"Because I need something bad in Honiara, and I gotta stay here to get Rua, my daughter. You understand?"

"Damn, yes. We all with you. Daughter damn important, you sleep at night."

"Who else comes here? Quietly? No record."

"Some smugglers, maybe."

"Okay," I said. "Don't tell me anything more. Got a dangerous deal for the smuggler."

CHAPTER FORTY NINE

What I Need
or
Dealing

While his sailors cussed and slammed tunny fish and copra in Styrofoam coolers into the hold, I muttered my order to Big-Man.

"Nobody touch dis damn stupid idea, yours," he said.

"You have to sail. I have to try."

"Get on *Laura Nyro* with us. Call American diplomatic from Honiara. I see movies, they send everyone, FBI, CIA, United States Marines to rescue one White girl virgin."

"You're watching the wrong kind of movies, Captain. Those are Hollywood feel-good yuppie fantasies. D'you know what will happen if I tell the State Department that my daughter Rua is with Ugi?"

"Damned know."

"Some clerk will ask me for date of birth and any proof that Ugi kidnapped Rua. And who saw it. And did I make a police report? Rua is not a minor, so she is not a runaway. They'll forward my complaint to Washington and keep it on file in case Ugi ever tries to kidnap the Pope. Meanwhile, Ugi kills us, maybe Rua too and the Prime Minister here keeps him cool with a political job as Cultural Advisor On Ethnic Tensions."

"Maybe occur in that manner. But this smuggler, very serious type. If I get him in trouble, set him up, somebody, his friend, kill me."

"There's no setup here. I'm just making a deal, like Monty Hall."

"Have this Monty Hall make deal for you. Is safer."

"Can't. Dead Monties make no deals."

"No. Cannot ask this. Risk too big."

"Captain, you just saw me risk my life to help your sailors. That Oscar, there. He's a character. Him and his tongue."

"Cannot do it. Risk my damned life and ship so you can play American Johnny Wayne."

That seemed flat. My luck was out.

Rua would die in some cross-fire here. I would have to tell Diana.

"Marau Island looks dangerous to me now," I said. "We can't guard the shoreline all the time. Ugi can land his radical boys whenever and wherever he wants. Use the jungle for cover and crawl right up onto our collarbones. Kind of like the Japanese on Guadalcanal. Now I know how those kid Marines felt."

My dreams came back to me but I shook them off. Now was the time to stay focused.

The Captain had already forgotten our talk.

"Hey, you sons of one-night-stands gone bad!" he entreated. "You play with being dead, work lazy so that Ugi come back in time to shoot you like anything!"

"Hey, Cap," I said. "D'you know Laura Nyro's most mysterious song? Ya got me interested in Laura Nyro so I checked the Web and found a piece about one song. And I learned to sing it for you. They call it Laura Nyro's most mysterious song."

Again, I was lying. Years ago, I had learned and liked this song. Laura Nyro only recorded it once. The Captain would not know it. Few people would remember it. I would lie forever to get Rua back.

"What means 'mysterious'"?

"Inscrutable. Enigmatic. The song that nobody can figure out."

"No. Damned know it."

"It's called 'Christmas in My Soul'. Came out in her album, *Christmas and the Beads of Sweat*. That song is probably the only radical Christmas song ever written. She seems to agree with the radicals of her time in 1969. She calls the Black Panther on trial for murdering a policeman one of God's sons. History shows us that the Black Panthers were just thugs and killers, spouting revolutionary talk to fool naive idealists."

"Yeah?"

"You don't have that song on your collection. Want me to sing it for you?"

"Yes, please!"

"Maybe you should video me singing it? On your phone?"

"Smart, yes, good idea, how you trick me this way."

"Now, Captain. Really."

While the crew kept loading, I sang Laura Nyro's song from memory.

"Pretty music," Oscar said. He swayed to the music.

"Keep famous tongue inside mouth," the Captain said as he filmed me with his phone. He spoke in a whisper that my singing would cover. "Filthy animal."

The music reached Tattoos, who rarely smiled. He snapped his gnarled fingers. He was way offbeat, but it did not matter.

My voice pitched high and then low. At the end, I climbed up, rising the way that Laura did, praying that my voice would not crack.

My luck held.

"Beautiful music," the Captain said.

"Laura Nyro did it," I said. "Not Dancing Max."

"Pretty, pretty."

"She thought that her song could reform violent radicals," I said.

I was winging it. Nobody could be sure of what an artist was trying to do.

"If she can do it, we can do it," I said. "I'm going to get Rua away from Ugi, change his ways and teach dance here on Marau like I promised. Need your help."

He spat over the side.

Nobody spoke for a while.

"Okay, I do like you want," he said. "Can contact your dealer. Secretly. But if is problem, I will have someone interfere with you intimately, please Jesus your worship."

"Captain, your Latin is improving," I said. "And thanks for the trust. I won't forget it."

The Captain walked onto the boat, shouting.

To get near the Big-Man Saku, I thumbed at the Captain.

"Big-Man, why does he keep threatening them with sexual destruction?" I asked.

"Why do YOU waste time with frivolous enquiries?"

CHAPTER FIFTY

Sociology
or
The Japanese Soldier

Big-Man's face looked too adult when he queried me that query.

"Can I help load your boat?" I asked the Captain.

"Not now," the Captain said. "Better you keep watch Ugi, that troublemaker."

Big-Man Saku kept looking through me. Behind him, islanders slung sweaty burlap sacks into the hold.

"Ugi no good," one said.

"By the way, Big-Man Saku," I said. "Wanted to praise you on your manner of speaking."

"Don't try winning the cannibals over with fake praise. I took first in Political Science at University of the Pacific here on Guadalcanal. I prefer to lead my Malaitan followers through true *kastom*. This entire issue of pitting Malaitans against Guadalcanal natives is a false issue, designed to split us apart. I watch your BBC news. There are many such paper arguments in your democratic system."

"Too right you are," I said. "I count the fake issues like sheep to put me to sleep."

"In the eyes of your CNN world, we Melanesians do not really exist. No army, no impact anywhere. It is no help that we are Black. Rumors of cannibalism still float here. No outsiders are sure about the rumors. We are castoffs, with wildly colorful clothes and funny customs like shark-calling. The traditional way was to pound stones together, underwater in the harbor at a certain point in the year. The sharks would hear it and thrash towards the sound of the stones and cluster that way. They would crowd without attacking anyone."

"That's wild," I said, checking the water by reflex.

"Sharks are unpredictable."

"Not when we worship them, give them sacrifices and do not try to kill them for the shark fin soup like the Chinese do."

"That word 'sacrifice' worries me."

"It should not. It is all bound up in trust."

"An example, please."

"During this shark-calling ceremony, the Big-Man's son would enter the water with the sharks. Some of us cry out that he will be eaten. But, if he has faith in the worship, he swims to the largest shark fin and holds on. Then the shark takes him for a ride through the water. They dive and swirl together below the surface. When the boy needs air they break the surface and submerge again. This ride changes the boy and helps him to become a man. He never forgets this event."

"Guess not. Big-Man, have you actually seen this shark-ride ceremony yourself? With your own eyes?"

"About telling the truth, I am like Ugi, in this respect. So are many of us. We do not lie. No, I have not seen this."

"Okay, then," I said. "These are legends."

"So, you dismiss them? I'll tell you what is not a legend, Mister American. A soldier steals our food here on Marau Island."

"That happens, of course. Soldiering turns them wild. Wait a second. Solomon Islands doesn't have soldiers. No army. Just police. That's why the Australians are here."

"He is not a Solomons Islands or Australian man. He is Japanese. He has survived here since World War Two."

"Hey, Big-Man. You're tryna play Pin-the-Tail-on-the-Honky."

"A thousand pardons?"

"Tall tales. You're jerkin' my gherkin. A soldier left over here from the war would have to be in his nineties."

"Do you know your World War Two history?"

"Only in my dreams."

"For 30 years before the war, the prevailing theme was government by gunfire. Killers assassinated any vocal moderates. The ones calling for war convinced the Emperor that nobody could beat Japan. They subverted the true and honorable code of *Bushido* for their own political ends."

"That's why they sneak-attacked Pearl Harbor?" I asked.

"Partly. They feared your country's power to crush them. This soldier was brought up and reared to worship his Emperor as a god. It was not a valid political system."

"Then, I pity him," I said.

The crew kept loading the boat.

"Absolutely. He grew up in a propaganda cocoon. When he does not die in battle defending the Emperor, he and his family are disgraced. They would rather see him dead. This is the type of political naiveté that we seldom see anymore. The Internet would work against it. But he decided to stay. And he stole a rifle from us three years ago. Perhaps his own rifle had rotted away."

"It seems unbelievable," I said.

"It does not matter to me that you disbelieve me. But one's will can conquer anything, even when the person is in their nineties. We have Japanese and American veterans who vacation here, pitch a tent on their old battlefields and dig until they unearth a war relic. They return home happy. They, too, are over ninety. But they have the will. Do you have a strong enough will to find your daughter?"

CHAPTER FIFTY ONE

I Screw Up
or
Greek Fire

Laura Nyro kept singing about mercy on Broadway while the crew loaded the ship.

"We sing along, cause we know all the words," Redbeard grunted. "Captain, play it alla time, too much, yeah. Pound it into heads, us."

"Like advertising," I said.

"Like what?"

"Never mind."

The crew kept loading.

"Sorry to disobey your orders, Cap," I said. "But I gotta help these fellas load up. I want the *Laura Nyro* safe away from Ugi."

"Don't let El Capitan hear you," Oscar advised. "He in a bad mood now, got the red ass."

My airport bruises screamed some more as I strained to lift the copra sacks.

"Hey, you Yank, son of a one-night-stand!" the Captain cawed. "Damn't I tell you, watch for Ugi and his brigands? Bandit bastards play politics!"

"I'm better at loading than being Old Faithful Scout," I said. "Division of labor, Cap. The Henry Ford principle."

"Then you and Henry better obey your captain! I said, 'Watch!' So, you watch."

He clambered up to the wheelhouse.

I kept loading.

"Radio working here?" I asked Tattoos.

"Too far from Honiara. Captain cheap customer."

"What if you need help at sea?"

"We just go coast here. Open sea, no."

"Cheap captain, cheap radio," I said. "You get what you pay for."

We sweated some more. I would never get used to this heat. The jungle steamed just a few yards away.

"Cast off!" the Captain roared from the wheelhouse. "Get show on road!"

"Yayy!" Oscar crowed. "We're getting out of this mess!"

"Great!" I shouted. "You guys risked enough. See you in Honiara and I'll buy the drinks."

They pulled away from the pier and cleared the shoreline by fifty feet.

They turned left, heading west, towards Honiara. Big-Man Satu and I walked with the ship, keeping pace with the ship. He seemed to want to walk parallel to the *Laura Nyro*. Maybe it formed part of *kastom*. And I wanted him to teach me more about this place. *Laura* moved with dignity.

She did not look new or sporty.

"They'll get in radio contact soon," Big-Man Saku said. "And the Australian soldiers will mobilize here in gunships to seize Ugi and his group. Again, superior technology and numbers will win over revolutionaries. I must confess that I'm a bit conflicted by that."

"Ugi isn't," I said. "He wants to kill you."

"So he says."

"And everyone on your island."

"I merely confessed to being a bit conflicted."

Swimmers showed alongside the *Laura Nyro*.

Two heads bobbed.

"Where did those two come from?" I spat. "I was watching out."

"Sometimes."

"You mean, I didn't see them before?"

"Most likely, they were under the pier and just wait-ing," he said.

"Waiting for what?"

The lead swimmer hurled a plastic bag at *Laura*'s stern. The bag broke and sprayed liquid onto the water.

"AHOY, Captain!" I shouted.

"Too far. He cannot hear you."

The second swimmer flicked a plastic lighter to flame and tossed it onto the liquid.

Flames shot up from the water.

They trailed right to *Laura*. The stern smoked.

The two swimmers ducked down into the water.

"What's that?" I shouted.

"It could be any accelerant. Even gasoline."

"Nobody saw it!" I shouted. "Captain, you got a fire astern! Where's the man on watch?"

"This is not your navy, sir. They are just roustabouts that the Captain hires on a temporary basis."

The flames lit the stern.

Someone shouted.

The two swimmers showed their heads above water, about sixty feet from the boat.

The boat slowed.

The flames smoldered and then hissed out.

From a hundred yards away, I could hear the Captain cussing.

"She's wheeling about!" I shouted. "Why? He can make Honiara."

"He may lose his boat doing so. That fire lasted long enough to damage his stern. He might sink if waters turned choppy. No pru-dent boatman would take that risk."

"What did they use to torch the water like that?" I asked.

"Does it matter? Possibly, it might have been napalm. That floats on water. Ironically, you Americans first used napalm near here, fighting the Japanese."

"Here we go again, with the war stories," I said. "Wish it would get out of my head."

"Using fire to attack ships goes back in time. The ancient Greeks terrified the known world with a secret formula that floated on the waves and ignited immediately upon contact with any water. Historians called it 'Greek Fire.' The ancient alchemists kept the formula a closely kept secret. To this day, no man knows for certain how to create Greek Fire."

"Maybe our pal Ugi does." The Captain bellowed

"You can stop being conflicted now, Big-Man," I said. "As I said before, Ugi wants to kill us."

CHAPTER FIFTY TWO

Time Alone
or
Where's That Japanese Soldier?

The *Laura Nyro* swirled and slewed like she might go down right next to the pier.

"Bale this out, please Jesus your worship!" the Captain bawled. "We take water in the butt!"

"Stern, cap," I said. "Water in the stern."

"I beaching her," the Captain said. "Right now."

"Will hurt the hull," Tattoos said.

"Her sinking tonight will hurt the hull worse," I said.

We stood just a few yards apart, with me on dry land. We could talk to each other.

Showing skill, the Captain revved his engine to a horrible grinding noise and then pushed it out of the water and up onto the sand.

"Toss me a line, Cap," I said. "Can keep her tied to the pier so she stays at high tide."

"You was sailor before?" the Captain asked.

"Was everything before," I said. "But that's just common sense."

Giri came on deck.

"You can read this?" he asked.

He handed me a stained pamphlet stamped: *US War Department *** 1942*.

The book was an English- Pidgin-Japanese phrasebook with cartoons showing different things.

"You might need this, with the older islanders," Giri said. "Now, I must look at my engines. Maybe we can still leave."

"I just got an idea," I said. "Wiggy idea. How many people can this boat carry safely?"

"Big boat. Safely, calm seas, more than 100. Why?"

The *Laura Nyro* stayed half in and half out of the water. The crew scanned the burned stern, shaking their heads and looking grim.

"Captain, any of your crew been in any military?" I asked.

"Deserters, maybe."

"Any armies anywhere?"

"Jail?"

"No. Jail doesn't count. Big-Man, how many guns do your people have?"

"Why?"

"Because Ugi seems to have a lot of them. And he stopped the *Laura Nyro* because he wants to keep everyone trapped on the island. Run us off or kill us. Again, how many guns on your island?"

"Perhaps four or five," Big-Man said. "They are used for hunting of course. Not for fighting Ugi's war."

"That's going to change. Captain, you've three handguns and two rifles. At best. If you can fix them up to working condition. Your boat runs on diesel, right? That can burn, with enough oxygen. Tell Giri and the rest of your crew to start pouring diesel into any bottles they might have. Yes, even whiskey bottles. We'll need diesel gas bombs to throw if Ugi attacks us and we got less than ten guns total."

"Why do you give these orders?" Big-Man asked.

"To keep breathing. If someone else can do better than I can, put them in charge. But, until that time, I'm the boss."

"Why?"

"Because she's my daughter."

When they were all huddled around their engine, I slipped into the jungle, clutching my sword cane.

In case anyone noticed, I exaggerated my airport bruises limp on my legs.

That would explain the sword cane. This was not acting. Everything still hurt me. Older frames like mine took longer to heal.

Oscar was singing again. Then they joined in:

O! The monkeys have no tails in Samawango!

O! The monkeys have no tails in Samawango!

The jungle heat draped over me like a big dog swimming underwater. Trees blocked out the sun.

"We aren't going too deeply in here," I whispered. "Just enough to be hidden."

My feet mashed down some horrible-looking purple plants.

"And I'm talking to myself more and more since I hit Guadalcanal," I went on. "Either because there's nobody to talk to or I'm scoring more points in dementia-land."

Next to a fat tree with dried-out wood crevasses, I scooped out dirt to make a hole about four inches deep. An aspirin bottle said hello to $600 in twenty dollar bills and I wedged the cash inside and sealed it tight.

"President Andy Jackson," I said. "Guarding our twenties. Only President to ever murder a man in a duel. Crack shot. Andy, we need you now."

Bushes moved.

My heart slammed.

I flattened.

My sword slipped out of the cane.

It could be Ugi with an AK-47, burning to discuss Ethnic Tension with me. Or it could be Oscar, hiding in the jungle to point his tongue at female trees.

A flash of brown cloth showed a through the jungle.

It vanished.

Birds cawed more overhead.

Brown Cloth was disturbing them.

The movement stopped.

Adrenaline dumped me under a big tree's shade. After the swimming and fighting, my bones and cartilages needed to rest.

Stretching out, I scanned the phrasebook from my pocket. The Japanese words blurred.

My eyes got heavy.

I recalled the Japanese burp guns shooting in my dream. Now, in the jungle, the dream felt very real.

"Budda-budda," I mumbled.

That was the gun sound.

"Budda-budda," I repeated. "Just like counting sheep."

CHAPTER FIFTY THREE

Wandering
or
What I See

I woke up swimming in sweat.

My South Pacific clothes hung raggy on me.

Heat increased.

The sun position made it late afternoon.

It felt like I had slept for hours and my dreams sluiced back to me, with infantrymen in Marine greens or Japanese tan, both sides shouting in Nipponese or Cincinnati.

They kept echoing in my head.

Leaving the jungle, I saw the crew resting in shade near the boat. Laura Nyro sang a song from the Captain's phone. The Big-Man stood by with a group of women in flowered skirts.

"Music and boys and girls," I said. "Does anyone want a dance lesson?"

"Like to kick you underground," the Captain said.

"Guess you don't want a dance lesson," I said. "But I've got a new idea to handle Ugi."

"I damn't care of your new ideas to handle Ugi," the Captain said in a rare quiet tone. Somehow, that frightened me more than his usual tirade. "I tell you, watch for him. You damn't see his bought dogs kill my boat engine. Maybe I lose my boat, you."

"Not good, not good," Tattoos said.

"Supposed protect us," Oscar put in.

Oscar was nobody's idea of a serious committed professional. But he looked grave now.

"We have about nine old guns, not much ammunition," I said. Because the crew spoke a mess of polyglot English, Pidgin and their own languages, I had to avoid slang. "Maybe fifty men, able and willing to fight. Ugi could slaughter us with just two men and two assault rifles. But he's got much more. D'you jokers want to hear my idea?"

Calling them jokers formed a mistake. Police academy flashbacks were running my mouth.

"No, not from you," Giri said.

"Giri, I gotta ask you about ancient army tricks."

"No. Forget any talk. You let us all down."

Both my ears burned hot.

"Okay, friends," I snapped out. Showing my anger would be another mistake. "You hurt my feelings. I'm not gonna invite you to my birthday party, and now I'll go somewhere and just sulk."

"You go milk whatever you want to milk," the Captain said. "Just leave us. I am damned dumb, take you on. Not no more."

Like a kid, I stalked off.

When I was ten years old and suffering through Saint Blaise's School For Young Men, my teacher, Mr. McLaughlin, had always fascinated us by his talks.

Reaching far back, I tried remembering what he had taught about ancient warfare.

I ventured back into the jungle and looked at the *Laura Nyro* from here.

"Yup," I whispered. "Anyone attacking the ship would come from here. Everywhere else, the brush is too thick. There's swampy foul land to the left. Nobody would come through that. Fallen trees make another barrier."

I dragged some fallen rotted trees to where I wanted them.

"Here is their attack spot," I said. "Gotta be."

The point of my sword broke through the top layer of dirt. Then my mad took over and I dug until full dark.

It felt better than shouting at the crew.

Something ran past me in the brush. Whipping around, I saw a man's shape. His bare foot kicked up. He wore a poncho of some kind. Matted hair swung from his head.

"Kakamora!" I shouted. I was trying to get the crew here. He whipped around to stare at me. Then he bolted back into the jungle.

"Kakamora," I breathed out. "The lost race. I just saw one. Can't tell the Cap or the crew. Some may say that I'm making it up. I'll lose more respect. Can't risk that with our big fight coming up."

When I returned to the boat, nobody talked to me. They were eating with the Big-Man and the islanders. From the galley, I scored some kind of sweet crackers from Indonesia and canned peaches. Then I slept on the forward deck, exhausted.

The war dream came back to me.

"Maybe I'm finally cracking up," I whispered to myself. "Seems like the right place for it."

The next day, I walked the island and drew my own map of it.

Nobody asked me what I was doing. Nobody cared.

They kept singing about the monkeys in Samawango.

Two days passed like this.

My war dreams got worse.

CHAPTER FIFTY FOUR

Missing Machine Charley
or
The Adults Snub Me

"Everybody's snubbing me around here," I told myself on the third morning, sleeping a decent distance from the others.

By day, I worked on my digging with the sword cane and slept through war dreams afterwards.

On the third morning, a small boy brought me a tray of biscuits and honey, jackfruit, some odd-colored melons and steaming tea in a cup.

"What's this mess?" I asked as graciously as possible, coming from my combat nightmares.

"I bring you breakfast," he said in a slurred British accent.

"Bolshoi," I said. "What am I, the village leper? I eat with everyone else. If they don't like me eating with them, they can institute deportation proceedings."

I took the tray and strode over to the village guest house, made of wooden planks and a slanted rooftop. The crew was living inside it, Redbeard and Oscar draped over the porch.

"Good morning, all," I said. "Here to integrate your breakfast board."

"No, boss," Redbeard said. He clambered to his feet.

My senses screamed.

I had to step up.

"You better sit back down before something happens to you," I gritted out.

He waited.

Then he sat.

After sundown, a speedboat would buzz us on the island and fire bursts of full-automatic shots. They shouted

"Ugi rules!"

"This reminds us how many guns Ugi has," Big-Man said. "And unlimited resources for guns and fuel for the boat."

"Maybe we should just leave, then," a thick-built islander named Kebu said. "Get the Aussie soldiers to fight Ugi off our island. No need for a fight that kills us."

"How can you talk of leaving?" Big-Man asked. "Is life that precious to you? Marau is sacred land to us. We stay."

"One night, they come ashore and kill us all," Kebu said. An idea struck me. Speaking out might get everyone riled up against me. But I had to try. I was getting tired of hiding mute.

"You notice one thing about this speedboat with the gunshots?" I asked.

Nobody answered. They just looked at me.

"Who here remembers the war stories?" I asked.

No reaction showed.

The audience was sitting on their hands.

"That Japanese plane would keep its engine out of synch just to be loud and keep our boys awake," I pressed on. "The plane would drop a few bombs that never hit anything but the jungle. Our boys called him 'Washing Machine Charley' because of the engine's noise. Because our speedboat gunner always misses, we should call him 'Missing Machine Charley.' What d'you say to that?"

Giri snorted.

"I think that you are deranged," Big-Man said. "And troubled in your head."

"Trying to make a ha-ha funny as men want to kill us," Redbeard said.

"That's right when you need the ha-ha funny," I said.

"Missing Machine Charley," Oscar repeated.

That night, the speedboat showed again, firing shots.

"He may want us to waste bullets shooting back at him," I said. I was thinking out loud. "We have no chance of hitting him at night, at this range. Or Ugi may want to test our firepower, by counting our guns."

"You was army, Yank?" Tattoos asked.

"I wish," I said.

Maybe they forgot that they were shutting me out.

"Ugi rules!" Missing Machine Charley shouted from his speedboat, about two hundred feet out.

He fired a burst at the island.

Some of us flinched.

"What matter, we stay or go?" Kebu said. "Solomons Islands mean nothing, nobody, nowhere. Not America, Russia, China. We just a place, get fish. Copra. Why we stay, this Marau Island?"

The Big-Man unloaded a mess of words on him. It might have been the Are-Are language and it sounded pretty rough.

Missing Machine Charley left and I could see the white cream of his wake in the blue-black half light after sunset.

"I know, I know," I said. "You kinda miss Missing Machine Charley when he goes away."

"You crazy, dude," Oscar opined.

The waves kept lapping the beach before us. The *Laura Nyro* stayed still in the light.

Everyone talked and smoked.

Kids played by the water's edge.

A different boat engine sounded. This one was smoother than Missing Machine Charley's boat. It was heading straight for us.

"The attack coming," the Captain said.

Giri hoisted the Lee-Enfield and Redbeard picked up the .22 rifle. Someone had fixed the stock and used electrical tape to keep the rifle together again. The fixer had done a miracle of repair work.

"The final attack," a woman said in a British accent, face hidden in the dark. "But we will not run."

"Ugi could land more gunners anywhere," Giri said. "Just like the war."

The boat stopped at the pier.

I felt like screaming.

A woman in a bikini came from the boat, with a long gun.

Someone fired.

CHAPTER FIFTY FIVE

New Guest
or
Lust Conquers All

The woman dropped.

"O, showers of bastards!" I shouted. "Don't shoot!"

"Bloody idjits, with guns!" the woman cried out.

I knew the voice.

"Guns down!" I shouted. "She's a friendly!"

"It's Elie!" the woman shouted. She sprawled on the pier, one long leg exposed from her dress. "Bringing this gun to Max!"

"Who is Max?" Tattoos said. "No Max!"

"Fat old Yank, Max!" Giri hollered.

"Thanks," I said.

"Why do you bring gun out like that?" the Big-Man asked. "Why not wrap it in something?"

"Like what?" she said. Someone lit her up with a flashlight. Even now, she looked lovely and angry to me in a tight jade-colored sheath dress. "Wrap the gun in my dress and come here naked?"

"In that dress, it would not matter much," I said. "And I heartily approve."

"What you say?" Oscar asked.

"Whatever it is, she's got it," I said. "That's what I said."

Elie let the submachine gun lie on the pier and stood up straight. She showed her hands and raised them slowly to her shoulders. It looked like a slow dance of surrender and it worked. The men stopped thinking about fighting and the women watching from their huts shook their heads. The women probably saw Elie as a brazen modern hussy, trying to steal their men.

"Elie, you came out here alone, with the gun?" I asked. "And in that dress?"

"Got my clothes packet here, to change. I wanted to make a good appearance for my lover."

"Sure," I said. "Whoever he is."

"You, darling."

That rocked me.

"Don't you remember?" Elie asked. "Are you suddenly ashamed of me?"

"Play your game for now, Elie. What about the gun?"

"Papa Ting said that I was the only one he trusted to bring you the gun and get the money owed. I convinced him that I could handle anything."

"I bet. Including him."

"Known me since I was a little girl. I could never cheat him. And I've been piloting speedboats like this one forever."

"I'm mad confused, Elie. How did he know that I needed this Tommy gun here and now?"

"Don't know. He just knew."

"This doesn't make sense. Too many mysteries here."

"You owe seven hundred dollars for the gun," Elie said. "Carrying case and three extra bullet clips. A free knife from your Marines. I never knew Papa Ting to be so generous. Plus, two hundred more for delivery."

"Not that generous. Why two hundred more?"

"Fuel for the boat. And because I took holiday from my job for this. Nothing more. I come free."

"We'll leave that alone."

"This gun not *kastom*," Kebu said. "Not good for us to have here, Marau."

"Kebu, you're starting to sound like what behaviorists call 'a toxic personality.' If this Thompson, designed in 1918, bothers you that much, Ugi's got some more modern weapons that will really make you disapprove."

The Captain stood with the Lee-Enfield carbine in his hands.

"Cap, how did you get my gun request to Honiara so fast?"

"What gun? I damn't see no gun. You buy something, you pay. Okay? No questions, me."

"Well," I said.

Elie chattered at Big-Man in Pidgin, too fast for me to grasp. She handed me the Thompson with a canvas carrying case holding the ammo drums and a wicked-looking knife. The brown knife sheath had the US Marine Corps globe-and-anchor insignia on it. She led me to a grass and wood shack a few yards from the others. She carried a pink backpack with the Australian flag stenciled across the top.

Nobody was in the shack. A long flat mattress lay on a wooden board. I could see a few blankets in the darkness and nothing else. I hoped that no kids were hidden here, watching.

"I've been sleeping on the ground outside," I said. "How do we rate this?"

She pulled me to her and kissed me long and hard on the mouth. I felt my control start to spin away.

"Let's cancel the theater right now," I managed to say. My chest heaved. "We aren't lovers. And, if I read my own signals right, we aren't going to be."

"Seven hundred dollars. Plus two hundred more."

"We'll sleep on it."

"Max —"

"I said tomorrow. Just before you and your speedboat depart."

"Why should I go? Remember, I'm on holiday."

"Some holiday," I said.

"And you're more exciting than serving SolBrew beers to dirty rice farmers."

"Yeah? And just who are you working for?"

"I don't understand."

"Dorris and the local cops aren't swift enough to put an officer undercover as a barmaid. But they might use you as their informant, short-term. Sometime, after pillow talk, you cut my wrists and make it look like a suicide. Despair over impotence or something else."

"Hmm. Suspicions?"

She wrapped her limbs around me until I could feel her breathe. My body tingled.

We sank down onto the mattress.

CHAPTER FIFTY SIX

Escape Try
or
The Sea Takes Back

"I don't care what you say!" Oscar's voice said the next morning, waking me through heavy rich sleep next to Elie in my shack "I'm going!"

"Why do you get up?" Elie mumbled in her British accent. She lay sprawled, Black and naked and strong and lean, alongside me on the mattress. "We have more tricks to do."

"I bet we do," I said. "Right now, I got family responsibilities."

"Ohhh, poooh!"

Throwing on my shorts and T-shirt, I tottered outside and down to the pier.

Oscar was inside Elie's speedboat. The Captain, Big-Man the crew and islanders tensed up nearby.

"You stealing gal boat," the Captain said. "And deserting *Laura Nyro*."

"I send back Aussies soldiers," Oscar said. "Keep us all alive."

"The woman does not need her boat now," Big-Man said. "She is using a different transportation systems, that is, her loins, hoping to transport herself to become an American wife-citizen."

"Is that what she's doing?" I said. "Wonder who that American is."

"Talk too much," Oscar said. "I go."

He revved the boat engine and cast off from the pier.

It was mid-morning, about eight, judging by the heat.

"Know that boy long time," the Captain said. "Got drunk, catch women with him. He never plan. Always get trouble. No plan."

"Today, his plan of 'no-plan' just might work," Big-Man said. "I pray."

Oscar's boat sped out and turned left. It was the same route we had taken with the *Laura Nyro*.

"He must stay close to the shoreline," Big-Man said. "That boat is not capable of surviving high seas farther out in the water."

Another boat, a new one painted orange and white, came out fast from shore.

"Where was he hidden?" I asked.

"There are many coves along the shoreline," Big-Man said. "We cannot see them from here. Ugi could hide twenty boats and a thousand men there and the jungle being so dense, we would never know."

"Oscar not escape that one," Tattoos said. "Look how he is moving now."

Oscar's boat seemed to strain, trying to pull away. But the other boat crested over the flat waves and drew within twenty feet of Oscar. The island women keened. They sensed trouble.

One Black man stood at the wheel. His arm came up and something spun end-over-end at Oscar's boat.

The something hit Oscar's bow. Flames flared.

"Fire-bomb!" I shouted. "Oscar, get in the water!"

"He goes in the water, they will run him down," Big-Man said. He startled me by lighting a cigar. He did not seem like a smoker. Maybe his nerves made him smoke. "Better that he can put out that fire himself."

Oscar went forward, spraying something on the flames. The boat spun. Wind whipped flames onto his pants leg. He screamed. His shirt caught fire. He jumped overboard. The boat exploded. It caught him in mid-jump. Debris slammed his body.

He hit the water and stayed still. Nothing moved.

"Boy is gone," the Captain said. "Cannot live, that."

I felt like throwing up.

The killer boat turned towards our pier and approached. It was Ugi, alone in the boat. Maybe Rua was ashore somewhere or maybe she was already dead.

Ugi stopped about fifty feet from us. He waved a white rag as his boat heeled up in the water.

"This is a flag of truce!" he shouted. "Will you honor it?"

"You just killed a boy!" Big-Man shouted. His cigar smoke plumed.

"Will you honor it?" Ugi repeated.

"YASS!" the Captain shouted. "Is okay. Talk."

"I just used fire to neutralize an enemy," he said, using his voice's normal volume. "Fire was always the weapon of Ugi's party, using direct action. Anyone can use a gun. Fire is mobile, inexpensive and found everywhere. Democratic. You may smell your own skin burning if you ignore our revolutionary progress and stay on this wretched island. You and your children will live better in Honiara. Better jobs, schools and medical care. Why do you insist on staying here?"

"It is our home," Big-Man said.

"A modern, caring parent should make a new home, if it helps his family," Ugi said. "But there's another reason. I'm tired of sexing this White woman living with me. I have used her enough."

His voice made me wonder about Rua. Maybe Rua was a wild lover.

Years ago, her mother Diana had worn me out. Maybe hot blood was genetic. She was my daughter, too.

"If you remain stubborn and traditional, for no real reason," Ugi went on, "her blood is on your hands."

Big-Man reached into his shoulder bag, gripped a glass soda bottle and touched his cigar to the mouth. Something sizzled. I smelled gas.

"Careful!" I shouted.

The bottle flamed. Big-Man flung the bottle straight at Ugi's boat.

CHAPTER FIFTY SEVEN

Rules Of War
or
My Plan

Ugi must have been poised and waiting for something.

The fire-bomb flew twenty feet towards Ugi. Big-Man threw it like he had hunted birds with stones as a child.

Ugi batted the bomb away.

It burned his hand.

"Yow!" he shouted.

The bomb flamed and pitched into the sea.

Ugi shook his burnt hand.

"You use fire, then we use fire against you!" Big-Man shouted. He had never lost his cool before. "Same kind of bomb, to kill you."

"You just violated a flag of truce," Ugi said. His voice pitched serene and mellow. "That breaks the rule of law. That means that there are no more rules now. I'm going to have this silly little island for my people or have you all exterminated."

With his good hand, his left, he turned the boat around and sped west along the shoreline.

"That was a stupid move, Big-Man," I said without thinking.

"I broke my word, yes," Big-Man said. "Though it was the Captain who agreed to the truce, I did not speak up. I acquiesced."

"Breaking your word is not *kastom*," I said.

"You are correct. But if Ugi dies, the Ethnic Tension loses its more potent leader. Nobody can create chaos like Ugi can. Nobody can reach so many disaffected Guadalcanal folks as he can. So, if this is war, I acted like a commander on the front lines."

"Foolishly. If we had expected any consideration from Ugi before, we can't now," I said. "We gave him the perfect excuse to wipe us out."

"You talk like a woman," Big-Man said.

"I hope so," I said. "A smart one. I know a lot of women too wise to do what you just did."

Something moved in the bush. It was light brown cloth. Sunlight caught steel and then it was gone.

"That same guy!" I sputtered. "Right there! Look!"

None of them moved fast enough. They were looking at jungle.

"It's someone I saw before!" I said. "All by himself, in the bush."

"It is no matter," Big-Man said. "I've seen him for years. He is our Japanese soldier. Now, do you believe us telling you about him?"

"After I talk with him, I'll believe it," I said. "Not before. He could be some mental case who thinks that he's a Japanese survivor."

"Oh?" the Captain said. "You don't know."

"Time to hear my plan," I said.

"Not now," he said.

"Yes, now! Ugi has to hit us soon, before Ting puts out an alarm for his boat or somebody needs the *Laura Nyro*."

"Could be a week," the Captain said. "We not busy."

"Ugi has to move before any Aussie soldiers check on us here," I said. "Here's my plan. Instead of defending each house, everyone crowds into the *Laura Nyro*. We use that as our fort, our base. We use logs and sandbags to keep bullets out. And as long as we hold the boat, we hold the pier. It's the only place on the island with enough clearance for the Aussies to land a big airship with troops. Right, Big-Man?"

"Two years ago, they tried landing Red Cross workers by helicopter in a typhoon on our south coast," Big-Man said. "They could not do it. The brush was too thick. They had to land on our concrete pier here. So, you're right about that."

"But your idea is ridiculous," he said. "We should form small bands and attack Ugi at our leisure."

"With our less than ten guns?"

"War clubs," Big-Man said. "Spears. They don't make noise and they don't malfunction. In thick jungle that we know and they don't, we will see them first and attack."

"Your islanders aren't soldiers," I said. "Farmers and fishermen. Some of us, sailors. Forget that American Revolution fantasy about the Minutemen and embattled farmers. Pros always beat amateurs. And Ugi got some pro thugs."

"What if they torch the boat, since Ugi likes fire so much?" Big-Man asked.

"We shoot anything that comes near us," I said. "That means that we only have to defend a boat that's how big, Captain?"

"One-one six feet long," the Captain said.

"Instead of defending almost two hundred islanders here, in houses spread out a quarter of a mile. We can't defend that. We can defend the boat, with us inside it."

"No mo *tok-tok*," one of the women said. "*Waytii mann* off his blooming chump."

Other islanders nodded.

"You do this crazy idea, save your daughter?" the Captain asked.

"It's not crazy," I came back. "It's our best plan. On board the ship, we have water and food for a month. If we go into the bush, we'll have to carry it. Ugi will have to carry his own supplies to keep us penned up. And when was the last time any of you slept outdoors in this jungle? Dealing with rain, jungle rot and malaria? Let Ugi deal with those problems while we stay safe in our boat."

"You go," the Captain said.

His tone chilled me.

"You get us all dead. Give you gun, food, water. But you leave us now. Go, *waytii mann*."

CHAPTER FIFTY EIGHT

Talking
or
Remember the Laura Nyro

The Big-Man and the sailors and the islanders all grunted and slapped their bare bellies. That was probably some sign of approval.

The Big-Man put my doubts to rest.

"You should go now," Big-Man said. "Today. PDQ. You don't need a rifle since you have your own automatic weapon. The Captain was just being generous. If you stay, someone might shoot you by an unhappy accident."

That shook my hands some. I jammed them into my pockets of the shorts so nobody could see.

"Okay," I said. "I'll go. But see that field there, to the left? Nobody should walk there."

"Why not?"

"Because that's how Ugi will approach you. And I dug dozens of foot traps in that field, to slow Ugi down."

"Foot traps?" the same woman asked. She wore henna in her hair, over a strong face and a worker's stout body.

"Giri, you know them from your military history," I said. "Foot traps are holes dug into the ground. Loose grass or brush covers the hole. When the soldier steps on the covering, his own weight breaks the grass covering. One foot is inside the narrow hole. He will panic and try to yank his foot up. But he can't. The foot is wedged. He is stuck there for a while."

"It won't accomplish much," Big-Man said.

"I also cut branches, sharpened their points and wedged them into the sides of the trap, pointing downwards. If he pulls his leg out, the points will break the skin and make his leg a bloody mess. But that's not the important part."

"What is?" the Captain asked.

Now I was going to lie. For a divorced man, I had never learned the craft like others did.

"Laura Nyro wrote a song called 'Remember the Alamo'", I said. This was my Big Lie. "She praised their courage in 189 of them standing up to 4,000 Mexican soldiers for their own freedom."

I was not going to say that the Alamo defenders wanted to have slaves on their farms. This was the wrong audience for that plank.

"They wanted freedom from Mexico's harsh rule," I said truthfully. "Like Ugi plans for you, if he takes over. D'you think that Ugi plans to hold free elections? He will set himself up for life, like Castro or Mao. And those Texans needed to keep the farms that they had made and sacrificed for. The Mexicans attacked the Alamo and killed all of them. But in the weeks that followed, the Texans chased the Mexicans, shouting 'Remember the Alamo!' And the Texans finally caught the Mexicans by surprise and defeated them."

"Come on," Big-Man said. "This talk wastes our time."

Lying hurt me. At the same time, Laura Nyro was dead and my daughter, Rua Calia Josephsen, was still alive. At least, I hoped that she was.

"Captain, you and I are old," I said. "We will die sooner than we think. Maybe tomorrow. Few will remember you and I. Who remembers Laura Nyro now? She has been dead for twenty years. But, if we fortify your boat, make it strong against Ugi and fight him here, all over the Pacific, sailors will shout 'Remember the *Laura Nyro*!'"

"Because we die?" the Captain asked.

"Because we took a stand and shouted 'Remember the *Laura Nyro*!' It almost sounds like 'Remember the Alamo.' Can you think of a better way to keep her memory alive?"

"This is nothing good," Kebu blurted out. "You make dis captain crazy like you. Go now!"

He yanked out a bone dagger and stepped towards me.

CHAPTER FIFTY NINE

Knife Work
or
Debate

Cut victims knew what a knife could do.

I was a cut victim, years ago.

Remembering it, I froze.

Karate moves against a knife would get you killed.

Nothing worked in close like this.

"Old Kebu," I croaked. I strained to make it sound like we were old sports-bar buddies, pounding down Harvey Wallbangers and rooting for the Brooklyn Cyclones baseball team.

It did not work.

He came closer.

"Old Kebu," I said. "Perhaps you and I are not communicating well here. What is it that you want me to do?"

Questions from me could slow a roadrunner down.

The Captain reached his own hand down to his Civil War revolver. I had no idea what he wanted to do with it.

As an amateur, he might shoot both of us, maybe by accident. It would make a mess.

"You go," Kebu said.

"Can I take my gun with me? Or will you steal that, too?"

"I never steal."

"Okay. Then I'll go. You don't need to push. I'm leaving."

He and the knife stayed still.

"Yep, I'm going," I went on. "With my gun and ammunition. But I might get angry at you later on. Creep back here at night. Holding the gun. Seeing you drinking tea at night, still mad at you. Is that what you want?"

"Then I kill you now."

I always talked too much.

"Then, what? Kill me, no reason? After you kill me, will you steal my gun?"

Repetition might work.

"Tell you, I don't steal."

"Then, you're killing me for no reason. And someone has to take the gun. Everyone will say that you killed me for the gun."

"No. Not that."

"Then, why?"

"Because you won't go."

"This is getting silly. I told you I'm going. Maybe we can forget the whole thing. Huh? I'll forget it if you will. Okay? You gotta brain and I gotta brain. We don't need the knife routine."

"You go."

"Captain, my plan just might save your boat. But if we leave the boat here and fight in the jungle, Ugi will sure as hell burn your boat just to show his power."

"Brother Kebu," the Captain said, "what Yank says makes sense."

"No, it don't."

Kebu was right.

I was gobbling word salad at him.

"Kebu, we need all damn fool fight this pederast Ugi," the Captain said. He took a deep breath, like someone deciding what to do. "Remember the *Laura Nyro*!"

His words hung in the air. Then he smiled. He seemed to savor the words.

Kebu whipped himself to the left and stalked away. He still held the knife. Maybe he was confused about what was happening. I know that I was.

The Captain showed no confusion.

"Hey, you products artificial insemination!" he cawed. "You know my name! My name Mrugank! You work, make this damn boat bulletproof or I dirty your private parts!"

Leading by example, he picked up some sandbags on the pier and carried them to the boat.

I tried to get my breathing back to normal. It did not work.

I sat down on a plastic chair and shuttered my eyes.

Elie came out of the shack, wearing a red T-shirt and tight white shorts, with her hair loose and heavy over her left shoulder.

"Couldn't sleep?" she asked in her accent.

"You were never more wrong."

"I thought that last night would keep you asleep till noon."

"Bed's a funny place," I said. "Not like ha-ha funny. You can never tell what's going to happen next."

"Really?"

"Let's find the biggest breakfast imaginable and eat it."

We did. Star fruit, hot biscuits, taro, fish and rice went down fast. We did.

Elie listened to the morning events and kept shaking her head.

"I was frightened enough bringing you that gun," she said. "But I've been piloting boats since I was little. The water doesn't scare me. Ugi does. Don't want to die this way. My Lord, nobody cares about the issues anymore. It has become tribal. They just ask, are you with Ugi or against him?"

Redbeard shouted something from the boat.

"Stay here," I said.

Others were jumping around the pier.

I leaped for my shack, got inside and snagged the green canvas bag. It felt clumsy. I tripped hauling it towards the ship, picked myself up and tried to run.

Speedboats lanced in from Ironbottom Sound. Red flashed. They were shooting at us.

My crew ducked and ran. Not good.

I dropped down behind a fat bent tree and yanked the Thompson out.

"New York cops never taught me this piece," I panted.

The safety on this gun was a mystery. But, as a kid, I had a toy model Tommy gun made by Mattel. The toy had a safety, a bolt you pulled back and a full-auto switch.

The boats kept shooting.

I hoped that my toy was the same as the real one. My gizzard depended on it.

CHAPTER SIXTY

Skirmish
or
I Fall To Pieces

Ugi's boat kept coming in.

"AWWWW!" Kebu shouted. "Ugi kill us all!"

"Shut up!" another hollered.

Panic could get us all killed, me, first. I always went to pieces in panic.

Full auto bullets flew.

One Islander toppled backwards, shouting "Argh!" He had no face. He flopped and lay still.

Another tugged the bolt on his hunting rifle and aimed at a boat. Thugs saw him and fired.

He waited and then pressed the trigger. In the boat, someone fell.

"Remember the Laura Nyro!" the Captain shouted from his wheelhouse.

Redbeard fired the Lee-Enfield carbine at the boats. Water nipped in front of the boats. He was shooting too high.

"Kill them now, our most best chance!" the Captain wailed.

Maybe Tattoos was hiding out somewhere. He liked Ugi, I remembered.

"Tommy gun's short range," I whispered. "Wait."

Women screamed past. They hoisted their kids onto the *Laura Nyro* and into the hold. Slugs hit the deck near them.

"Kill them!" the Captain shouted. "Is our only chance!"

Ugi's thugs were shooting from bouncing boats on a rough sea. Some shots went everywhere.

"Ugi rules!" they shouted.

I pushed my body into the ground behind the tree and sighted on the closest boat.

The boat got twenty feet out from shore, fifty from me.

I braced and tried to squeeze my trigger. Snatching a trigger always made me miss. The gun went BOP! BOP! BOP!

Nothing hit the boat. Maybe I was too high.

I lowered the gun and fired.

Black holes showed on the boat's port gunwale. One thug dropped.

Maybe I hit him. Maybe he ducked.

The boat pilot spun them away from shore.

A second speedboat reached the *Laura Nyro*. Ugi stood up in the prow and flung a firebomb at our deck, ten feet away.

"Burn you dead!" he shouted.

The firebomb hit. Flames showed.

Giri came forward and sprayed the flames with a red tank in his hands. White powder flew. The flames burned.

One thug stood up to hurl another firebomb. He was touching our hull.

Tattoos burst from the hold and threw a spear at the thug.

Ugi went low and rolled away, six feet out of the way.

The spear flew true and hit the thug center mass in his chest.

The thug swayed.

He gripped the spear in both hands and dropped down. He stayed still.

Away from him, Ugi shouted something.

I tried for Ugi. He was gone flat in the boat.

I swept shots across two other boats.

They wheeled about and retreated.

Another islander cartwheeled down. He held his leg.

The Captain's Civil War gun bucked in his hand.

"Morphodites!" he screamed. "You know my name! My name is Mrugank!"

The boats whipped around and zigzagged. I aimed and fired a short burst.

With just four drums, I had to save my ammo.

"They going, please Jesus your worship!" the Captain screeched.

Flames kept burning on deck.

"They come back," the Captain said. "We lucky this time."

CHAPTER SIXTY ONE

The Japanese Soldier Just Kibitzes
or
Scheming

Ugi's boats passed out of the cove, past the barrier rocks.

The same soldier in his tan uniform stood just inside the jungle. He might be the one everyone called the Japanese. He stood near where I had buried my cash and designed the foot traps. I wondered if he had been watching me fix my traps.

I slung my hot gun and checked a wounded islander. He was hit in the chest, a stringy man in his fifties, with betel-nut stained white whiskers and tattoos everywhere.

"What are you doing?" Big-Man asked.

"Make sure his mouth is open and he can breathe. Sometimes victims choke and die on their blood. Can you have everyone check? Even if they look dead."

"Morbid," he said.

"But necessary. Ugi's got more guns and we got women and kids. It's not a fair fight."

"Have you done this sort of thing before?"

"Never. That's why you're in charge, Big-Man. This is some weird dream fantasy, putting a city boy like me in a South Pacific firefight. Still can't believe I'm really trying to do this. Have absolutely no training or talent for any of this. I'm just here to try bringing my daughter back."

"Got two more dead ones here!" Redbeard sang out.

"We cannot afford even one," Big-Man said.

The Captain played a Laura Nyro song on his phone.

"Sounds like a rhumba, Cap," I said. "And we need it right now."

Elie crouched by a dead islander. She held a revolver.

My paranoia kicked in.

"Holster that!" I shouted.

"What?"

Reaching over, I gripped the gun barrel, moved it backwards and pressed the trigger guard against her fingers.

"Owww! Are you daft?"

"Let it go," I said. "Or I'll break your fingers. Maybe slice 'em off. Just open your hand."

She did.

"You're a sadist," she said. "I thought as much in bed."

"No side issues. This is a Smith & Wesson Combat Masterpiece, .357 Magnum. Where'd you score it?"

"A man gave it to me."

"I'll bet. A man named Ugi."

"No!"

"Or a man with a lot of gold braid, High Commissioner of the Royal Solomon Islands police. Swearing you in as a sex undercover. Department's secret weapon."

"Pardon?"

"It's a police gun. Civilians wouldn't buy it or tote it. Too bulky for what it shoots. Highway Patrols back Stateside still issue them as primary uniform guns."

"I tell you, a man gave it to me when he couldn't pay."

"I won't ask for what. It's in my gun bag now. If you need it, I'll toss it to you."

"You get us killed!" Kebu said to me from the deck. He poked a thumb at me.

"Kebu, are you married?" I asked.

"Seventeen years."

"Make it sound like jail.. Where's your wife?"

"There!" he pointed at a no nonsense stocky woman who was carrying an inner tube to the boat and making faces at it. "And she listens to me."

"I doubt it," I said.

Stepping over, I gave her my best Broadway smile and bowed a bit.

"Good evening, Mademoiselle Kebu," I said. "Your husband just told me so much about you."

I seized her into ballroom Closed Position and stepped forward into a rhumba step.

Kebu made a horrible grunting sound and closed his eyes.

Mademoiselle Kebu snorted a piggy little snort that went to a giggle.

"What you do?" she screeched.

"Like always. When in doubt, rhumba."

"Yank, why you cut the fool?" the Captain cawed. "Got work to do!"

"When Laura finishes, Cap."

Too soon, the song ended.

"Thank you, Mademoiselle Kebu."

"Is okay."

"Perhaps that dance changed your worldview. Dances sometimes do."

"We made mistakes," Big-Man said to everyone within range. Some were tending to our wounded. Others carried the dead. "We needed warning. From now on, someone with a rifle will watch the Sound all the time. Four hour shifts. If they see anything, a signal will be fired. Any unknown ships will be challenged and then shot at.

"We have four nurse's aides here. They also had extra training in wound care and CPR. They will wear red on their shirts and be grouped to help our wounded.

"Every person with a gun will have a 'shadow' with them. If the man with the gun is hit, the shadow's job is to take the gun and keep firing. Ugi must not be allowed to take the gun.

"Since Ugi has declared fire to be his weapon, I will make seven fire response groups to cover the boat. They carry water and sand. The Yank should have done this already. He let us down. Playing Daddy."

That steamed me. It was unfair. But, recalling my Police Academy days, when the trainer slammed you unfairly, you just sucked it up, buttercup. You never explained and never complained. Maybe Big-Man was establishing discipline.

"That's all for now," Big-Man said.

"Hey, Cap," I asked the Captain. "Need to know how you got my order for the Tommy gun to Papa Ting."

"Shut up!"

"Huh?"

"Or I hurt you!"

CHAPTER SIXTY TWO

Mysteries
or
What I Don't Know

"What?" I said. "Why you mad at me, Cap? Doesn't make sense."

I felt like everyone was putting the boots to me.

"You Yanks must to know all things always? You beg me, get word to Chinaman, you want big gun. Say, life or death. You think me stupid, tell me propaganda. So, I get message, Chinaman. My way, okay?"

"That's okay, Captain. And thanks again –"

"Thanks? Big gun maybe save your aged buttocks."

"Probably, Cap. I just need to know if Elie works for Papa Ting. Or does she work for somebody else? Like the police, part-time, maybe."

"You sleep her, you ask her."

"It's never that simple, Cap."

"Elie work for who, I damn't know. See you, laugh, sell drinks to my crew. Knows everyone, Guadalcanal."

"That's not much comfort, Cap."

"Find nice quiet place, self-comfort yourself."

He went back to yelling at his crew.

The adrenaline dump hit me and I sank down in the shade of a gnarled solemn tree. Someone had said the typhoon rains twisted these trees into weird shapes unlike any others in the world.

I felt the dump after shooting and maybe killing someone. That Thompson put out heavy .45 slugs, designed to kill. They hit harder and bigger than a 9mm round. Again, I wondered why I was shooting at committed radicals through an adult fantasy in a backwater eight thousand miles from home and logical living.

This was the kind of deal that I could never do well.

Different islanders were carrying furniture to the boat. They put the furniture against the windows to block Ugi's bullets.

"Mademoiselle Kebu!" I said to that hardworking woman dragging a dresser across the sand. "Hear that Laura Nyro song, 'Mercy On Broadway?' Let us dance to it."

"Why you always wanna dance?"

"Why doesn't everyone?"

"We just got shot at, Mister Dancing Yank."

"That's just why we should dance."

"I got work to do. I'm an adult."

She adulted herself away to her tasks.

"That just about sums it up," I said. "Sure are a lot of hardworking folks in the world and they tell me so all the time. That's why they're successful, and I'm just Dancing Max Royster."

Everyone was crossing from their homes to the boat, carrying children too young to walk. Elie passed by, carrying a cane chair.

"Elie," I said. "D'you hear that old Captain playing our song?"

We moved into dance position and stepped to a Laura Nyro tune, 'The Cat Song'.

"You almost broke my hand," Elie said. "Is that what women mean to you? Something to hurt?"

"You had a loaded piece in your hand. No reason to have it out since Ugi was gone, no training and a chaos scene with kids running around."

"Mister Right, with all the answers. You don't know anything about us. D'you know what it's like here, growing up Black and a woman?"

"Tell me. While we dance."

We danced. Nobody watched us.

"We live to be about fifty-eight years old here, on average," she said. "The Pacific average is seventy-two. Malaria takes us young. Have you seen our medical system?"

"Enough of it."

"I am Bageu, the tribe originally from Malaita's southeast coast. We grew up under the 'bride price' system. A boy sees the girl that he wants to marry and collects *Ta'Fuliae*. Those are polished beads with holes in them, strung around the neck and on a string. If he makes an offer to marry the girl, he must have enough *Ta'Fuliae* or else there is no marriage. We women have no say in this."

"How do they measure the shells?"

"In fathoms. That means six feet of shells on strings. A bride price may be as little as two fathoms. *Ro'Abala*, we call it. Some are thirty-five fathoms. Can you imagine that in your Yank mind? Different churches try to stop bride price because boys go into debt for life. But they can't change our culture."

"Ugi's trying."

"Ugi's trying to turn back history. He wants to make everyone use only bride price for marriage. No thought of choice or love. It will cripple us from ever going into the modern society."

"We have violent fundamentalists Stateside as well, Elie."

"Are they likely to kill you today? Because Ugi is. Last year, a lovely young New Zealand reporter girl came here to interview him for her magazine. Ugi brags how he used her for sex, ruined her career and made her homeless before she died in an accidental fire."

Hearing that, I thought of Rua lying naked under him and the shakes hit me. I folded into her, feeling the strength and the rich proud body held against me close.

"I'm fighting to look cool, in front of our allies here," I said truthfully. "But it won't work because I am just flat-out terrified."

CHAPTER SIXTY THREE

Siesta
or
Afternoon Heat

"It's getting even hotter," I told Elie as we carried planks to the boat. "Never knew what heat was until I came here."

"It's almost noon. Be sensible."

"Please explain."

"Watch the others."

The heat was slowing everyone down. They headed for their homes. Some went to the boat.

"Time for a kip," Elie said. "Let's have some privacy for the last time in our shack."

"How are all of us going to be comfortable in that boat?" I asked. "Don't tell me. I know. He'll kill some of us. Free up space real well, right?"

"Yank –"

"Maybe all of us."

Inside, we peeled off our clothes and lay on the floor. It amazed me how light clothes held the sticky jungle heat. When our bodies cooled, we started to hug.

Afterwards, I turned on my side and mumbled something like BUDDA-BUDDA.

I slept.

Later, we woke.

"Max, are you a Buddhist?"

"They probably wouldn't have me."

"Because you said some words in your sleep. Foreign. And called Buddha's name. Why?"

"It wasn't Buddha. BUDDA-BUDDA was a comic book sound for automatic weapons shooting in war. The artist would show some hero shooting a Tommy gun and write BUDDA-BUDDA in the box. It was like POW! or BAM! when something loud happened. Nothing to do with Buddha."

"And the language that you spoke?"

"Don't know. Was reading a Japanese phrase book the other day. Maybe it stuck in my head somewhere, somehow."

We woke again at sunset.

"I didn't plan to sleep all afternoon," I said.

She shot me a sloe-eyed look, under her heavy curling hair.

Outside, we carried some tin sheets to the boat.

Some islanders sneered at us.

"We're getting the hard eyes from everyone," I said. "Sleeping so late."

"They're just jealous."

"Some just."

"Carry this more evenly, can't you? Another helpless man."

"Elie, d'you want them to think that we're fighting?"

The wind, still hot, blew cooling breaths over us.

Bearded men in loincloths and wearing shell jewelry were sharpening ceremonial swords with wooden sheaths, testing the edges and hefting them. Tattoos shone with sweat. One man swung an ax. Another hurled his knife, sticking it into a coconut tree.

"Looks like the old world is going to war against the new," I said.

I could feel the fear everywhere. Some made hurried moves, others talked fast. They knew that time was short.

"Talk to them," Elie said.

"I'll try," I said.

Nobody saluted me as I approached.

"Remember to stay out of that field there," I said, pointing. "That's where I made those foot traps, to catch and cut up their feet. We want Ugi's thugs caught there, not our own."

"Dem foot-traps not gonna do nothing," a good looking full-bodied islander, with a goatee, about twenty said.

A group of island women swayed together by the water's edge, singing. The Captain shut off his Laura Nyro song, 'Lazy Susan', making a major sacrifice. The women seemed to be mourning something.

"Sounds like a hymn," I said.

Elie left me and barefooted her way down to the group. The men kept working, attaching tin sheets to the boat's hull and railings. It was starting to look like a patchwork design shirt with squares of tin, wood and plastic all quilted together to stop or slow down slugs.

Some women stopped singing the hymn and snapped at Elie. She answered back. They screeched at each other. The Pidgin went too fast for me.

"Don't sound like no hymn no more," I said. "What's the deal, Elie?"

"She a prostitute!" the smallest woman, round as a barrel, snapped. "Can't sing with us."

"Any of you got a direct phone line to God?" I asked. "Know real clear how He feels about things? Because, pretty soon, we may be talking to Him direct. No middleman. We could be graveyard dead anytime now."

"We know that, Yank," the round lady said.

"Then act like it."

They buzzed some more.

"I can take care of myself, Max," Elie said. "Stop trying to play the White savior."

"You're right. I'm wrong. Sorry."

They started singing again. Elie joined in. I was starting to feel like the White something or other so I left.

One man was testing a bow and arrow, bending the bow and sighting along it.

Mrs. Kebu used a flat gray whetstone to sharpen the edges of a shovel. She tested the edge with her fingertips, singing the same hymn from before.

Redbeard squatted on his heels near the boat's stern. He hefted a six-foot spear in his hands, with his pistol gleaming silver tucked into his belt.

"Can't sleep, boss," he said.

"Be surprising if you could. I probably can't, either."

"Why Ugi do this, boss? Make this mess?"

"Got no idea, partner."

"Why we gotta die on this little dumb island? Nobody gonna know."

CHAPTER SIXTY FOUR

Ambush
or
Try Dancing Through This

ACK-ACK-ACK!

Noise cracked me awake.

An ugly green helicopter flew above. I rolled away from Elie and one-handed, reached for my Thompson one-handed.

"Time for Budda-Budda," I said.

"Don't!" Big-Man said. "Look! She's Australian."

The helicopter banked. The Australian flag showed through gray morning fog.

"He's seen us all sleeping on a fortified ship," Big-Man said. "He knows that something is wrong, and he'll radio for help here. Our siege is over."

Guns fired in the jungle.

"Must be Ugi," Elie said. "Everyone else is bunched up here."

Slugs hit the helicopter. The pilot wheeled away. His plastic window blew out. The engine smoked.

More guns fired.

The helicopter exploded overhead. Debris rained on us. The copter spun crazy wild to left, circling. Flames ate her.

"Ugi's in the jungle!" Elie said. "Look! Coming here!"

I hoisted the Thompson to the gunwale. That steadied it. I saw nothing but jungle.

"Boats hitting us!" Big-Man said.

Whipping around, I saw speedboats coming straight at us. Guns showed.

"Attack from sea and jungle," I said. "Everyone, hit those boats!"

"Remember the *Laura Nyro*!" the Captain cried.

The singer Laura Nyro's song "Mercy On Broadway" blared out full blast.

My Thompson bucked. I fired at the lead boat. My slugs would not sink her. I had to kill the ones inside her.

"Remember the *Laura Nyro*!" a man near me shouted.

He notched an arrow into his bow and waited for a close shot.

As I shot, the boat came into my range. My slugs blew the pilot down. The boat swerved. I kept shooting. A man fell out. Another followed. The boat heeled over. Men dove underwater from it. Getting wet would not stop them. I had to keep shooting.

Other boats were already reaching shore.

"Remember the *Laura Nyro*!"

Redbeard fired the .22 rifle at another boat. Nobody fell. They fired back at him. Redbeard cussed and ducked behind a lifeboat, bleeding from the face.

I saw men coming through the jungle towards us. Ugi led them, acting like Castro taking Cuba. My Rua trailed Ugi, stumbling.

"Shoot slow," I said. "We're low on ammunition." I switched my gun to the jungle side. Ugi's men were moving right for my foot-trap field. In a minute, they would be in it.

"I surrender!" Kebu wailed. He jumped off our boat, hands high. "Ugi, don't kill me! Don't come any closer! They got traps there! Traps —"

Next to me, Big-Man cussed and lifted a long spear. He grunted and flung it at Kebu. It flew true. Kebu shrank from it. The spear hit his chest near the socket.

"Arghh!" he shouted. "Ugi, listen to me. I can help you —"

Mrs. Kebu came from behind the hull. She swung her sharpened shovel at Kebu's neck. He turned just in time to register what she was doing. Her whole body moved behind the swing.

Blood spurted in geysers.

His head rolled off his shoulders and hit the sand at his feet.

Others stared in shock.

From Patrol, I knew that cutting off a head was easy. Not much held the head to the body. You could do it with a razor.

Thugs came closer to my traps. I hoped that the fat leaves still covered them.

"How you do that?" Tattoos hollered at Mrs. Kebu.

"You!" she spat. "Do nothing. I hear you speak up for Ugi. Call him a patriot. That's why you're hiding now."

One thug went down in my foot trap, up to his shin. He tried pulling free.

"Awww!" he screamed. The wood spikes were working. Another thug got caught. A third dropped down into the ground.

Ugi fired his assault rifle. Mrs. Kebu slammed back against the hull. Rua screamed. Maybe she was learning that her radical lover killed women. I fired at Ugi too late. He was already behind a tree.

A firebomb burst on the deck behind me. The speedboats were throwing them. More bombs exploded. Ugi was keeping his word to use fire. A little girl caught fire, screaming.

Tattoos dropped the Lee-Enfield carbine and raced for the girl. He snatched the girl up, hugging her to his chest, smothering the flames. The flames died.

Thugs burst from the jungle and charged us, twenty feet away. Our spears and arrows flew. Two thugs fell. More kept coming.

Tattoos broke their charge. He grabbed up his carbine, fired shots and thugs dropped. He jumped from the boat, still firing. He ran to the first wave, reloading. One fell. Others shot Tattoos. He kept coming and fired again. Another spun down. Nothing stopped Tattoos. They saw this. They ran. Tattoos swung his empty rifle and smashed skulls. More thugs fled. Tattoos dropped to his knees, smiling. His eyes closed.

"Stop this!" Ugi shouted from behind his tree. Rua was tied to his hip by a rope. "Surrender or I kill this little White girl!"

CHAPTER SIXTY FIVE

Chances
or
Paternity

Behind me, our fire crew threw water and sand on the flames on the boat deck. The flames hissed and died.

I could not risk Rua's life now.

"Okay, Ugi!" I shouted. "You win! We surrender! Just let that woman go."

"No, Yank!" Big-Man said. "Don't surrender. We were winning. Look at his dead and wounded."

Dead thugs lay heaped around Tattoo's body. A dozen more thrashed, stuck inside my foot traps.

"The young lady enjoys my company for the time being," Ugi said. "Hear her."

"Ugi's just trying to stop the capitalist murder of Guadalcanal," Rua said. She looked more like me than she did Diana. Daughters resembled their fathers, sons took after their mothers. "Your soldiers and mercenaries firebombed his home, killing his family. You fear a White woman loving him."

Her voice carried some Carolina drawl with this propaganda.

"So, he must use whatever tools he can," she said. "Human Rights law justifies him."

Ugi's men watched, from the boats and beach. About twenty-five of them still stood free.

The Japanese soldier survivor stepped from the jungle, rifle slung.

It was time for me to act like a salesman.

"Ugi, I'm holding a US made Thompson submachine gun here, 50 shot drum magazine of .45 ammunition. May I surrender it to you?"

Let the customer think that he's deciding, I remembered.

"Or else I toss it in salt water and ruin it forever," I said.

Ugi pretended to think it over.

But every boy wanted a BUDDA- BUDDA toy.

"Yes, you may," Ugi said.

"Need my cane in the sand. I fell downstairs at Henderson Field."

LET HIM CORRECT ME. MAKE HIM FEEL SUPERIOR.

"Honiara International Airport, as we progressives call it," Ugi said. "Yes. You need your cane, old man."

"Don't do it," Big-Man said. "He's got to kill all witnesses now."

"I'm going up empty, Big-Man. Take the knife in my belt."

Big-Man took my Marine Corps K-Bar knife.

"When you return, I will kill you with this," he said. "Coward."

Thompson on safety, I tried to look as clumsy as possible, klutzing over the gunwale and landing on the wet sand, collapsing and hearing everyone laugh at me. My own side laughed.

If my farmers fired, they would miss Ugi, killing Rua and me. Only one guy here had the right training.

Rua was built lean and strong, like her mother. Her dark red hair riffled in the morning wind.

Ugi had her tied around her hips to him by a rope. He held a traditional bone knife at her throat, above her high young breasts.

I needed to distract him.

"I apologize," I said. "I did not understand that you are trying to help all Guadalcanal."

"How could you know?" Ugi asked. He was feeling generous. "The media lies about me."

Both of us were play-acting for Rua and everyone else.

"Here's the Thompson. I still owe Papa Ting."

I pushed it towards him, barrel up, with my left hand. I hoped he would sheathe his knife to take it. My right hand held the cane. I still had a sword up my sleeve. I hoped.

"Here, take it," I said.

"Just set it down. You were naive to trust me. I think that I will reinforce my discipline here."

My heart hammered.

"What?" I asked.

"Cut her anyway."

Rua screamed. He cut her throat skin.

I drew my sword from the cane, shouting something. It sounded like "*Hitojichi.*"

A shotgun fired behind me. Pellets hit my leg and the sword. My blade broke.

"Cheating?" Ugi said. "Watch her die."

A shot fired.

Blood burst from Ugi's bare chest. He choked. The knife dropped from Rua's throat. Ugi bent double. Rua broke free, crying.

"Ugi dead!" one thug with an AK-47 shouted. "Now they come for all us!"

He fled along the shore.

"Ugi dead!"

"Everybody run! Soldiers come now!"

The speedboats revved up and fled back to the Sound.

The Japanese soldier stood thirty feet away. He had shot Ugi. He worked the bolt action again. His lined face showed nothing. He looked like somebody's grandpappy, small and stooped and harmless.

"*Hitojichi,*" he said.

He turned back into the jungle and was gone.

Laura Nyro sang.

The Captain joined her.

Redbeard limped up, face bloody. He took the carbine from the dead Tattoos.

"I never gonna forget you, Khaleque," he said.

He scanned the thugs caught in the foot-traps.

"Go now," he said. "Or die."

"Help each other get free," I said. "That's real radical thinking for you. Go talk with the Kakamoras."

"Ah, you see the Kakamora finally." Big-Man said. "We see him all the time. Now you believe us."

"Max," Big-Man, using my name for the first time. "That word you said? What's it mean?"

"Means 'hostage.' In my Japanese phrasebook."

"You memorized it."

"Yeah. Hey, I'm bleeding here!"

"Who are you?" Rua asked.

"Rua," I said. "I'm your father."

Special thanks once again to…

To Detective-Investigators Mark Baldessare and Gerry McQueen and all the other cops and federal agents who taught me so much about hunting our real-life serial killers.

To the Spy, the Movie team – Jim MacPherson, Alex Klymko, Charles Messina and all the rest of the gang for a grand adventure in screenwriting.

To Nad Wolinska for her always inventive cover illustrations.

To Richard Amari for his equally inventive cover design.

To my screenwriting partner, Lynwood Shiva Sawyer, for his support and encouragement over the years.

To my talented editor, Michael Simpson.

If you enjoyed reading *Dancing Max Hits Guadalcanal or When in Doubt, Rhumba*, you'll definitely like Frank Hickey's other Max Royster novels

§

Love Finds Max at Christmas
or
Kissing in the Slush After Sixty

Frosty Manhattan Christmas. Our hero, Max waltzes with Peg, the mysterious beauty. A White cop kills an unarmed Black man and the city explodes in a night that goes on forever

§

The city throws a Unity Holiday Party, a dancing street fair to bring all together.

I, Max, 62, meet and flirt with a dark blonde beauty named Peg, a barmaid with no illusions left. Her looks and slangy streetwise talk hold me. At my age, she makes me smolder and feel 24 again.

No matter what it takes, I want her for mine.

But the plan smashes when a drunken Black man fights with a White rookie cop. The Black man dies and everyone hollers their own ideas about what really happened.

Seeing a chance to hit big on a settlement, I summon Nancy, a hooligan street-fighter with a lawyer's ticket. This kind of death means cash.

Peg is the only witness to the struggle between the drunken man and the cop. If I can run this, I can stop hustling forever.

Skip, another lawyer, Black, my nemesis-father figure, always scheming, hijacks Peg for his reward. His bodyguard, Joey, beats me in a fight.

The FBI and the radical group SAP-Stop Aggressive Police-jump into this case. Trying to out-dance them, I go undercover in SAP and live like a radical.

Through freezing stakeout nights and bitter dawns, I must find Peg and love at Christmas.

Max Wisecracks Hollywood
or
Foxtrotting for Justice

I, Max Royster, cannot run fifty yards or see my own feet under a beer belly.

Pushing sixty-four years old, I struggle to rebuild, after the New York cops fired me for depression and hijacked my pension.

Like everything else sliding around loose, I wind up in Hollywood, California.

§

By chance, I see a female Black LAPD cop grapple with a homeless woman, an ex-Blaxploitation film actress who 40-years ago turned Civil Rights radical.

The homeless woman dies.

Sidewalk Angelenos heave rocks and bottles in protest.

Los Angeles screams. Cops retreat and haul me to the station.

An ambitious Deputy District Attorney and the hard-charging FBI play witness tug-of-war over my fast-aging body. Everyone wants to jail me as a material witness for trial.

To stay clear, I go underground with a cryptic Hollywood beauty and learn much on the floor of her apartment. The media turns up the heat. The G-men freeze my cash.

All that I have left are my wits and the cash in my blue jeans.

When the Whistle Blows, Everyone Goes

Federal agents jail me for murder. That's me, Max Royster. Aging. Fat. Broke. And innocent. How do I clear myself from inside my cell? Nobody believes me. A hate group tries to rape and kill me. But Mother Royster always said to keep smiling no matter what. So to chase away the jailhouse blues, I organize a hipster group and swing dances among the inmates.

§

A Manhattan tycoon frets about his beautiful daughter.

She is cavorting somewhere near Palm Springs, California.

He pays me, Max Royster, to find her.

This simple job turns into a hairball.

She leads me astray.

Someone kills her boyfriend.

The U.S. Park Rangers blame me for it and lock me up in a federal prison.

Me being me, I try to stay cheery by organizing swing dances between male inmates.

An inmate hate group tries to rape and kill me.

Other inmates protect me for kicks.

Some enjoy the dances. Anything beats prison routine.

The warden and the correction officers suspect me of spying on them for the FBI.

Things look grim for our hero.

Can I swing-dance and laugh my way out of lock-down to find the real killer among the Beautiful People in Palm Springs?

Everyone wants to see what happens next.

You will, too.

Softening Flatbush

I, Max Royster, fat, broke, divorced, thrown off the NYPD for mental illness. Now in Flatbush, Brooklyn, I find new love, new murder and new career. Can I keep my love? Crack the case? Can I inspire and change private security? And maybe regain my NYPD shield?

§

Flatbush, Brooklyn, a neighborhood that used to be the borough's jewel.

Sixty years later, street crime plagues the area.

My love, Cooper, and her friends want to clean up the neighborhood and improve Flatbush's image. That way, they can 'flip' their homes and triple their profits

I join a security agency, thinking I can transform the guards from unhappy minimum wage-earners to passionate, hardworking crime fighters.

If I succeed and make Flatbush safe for Cooper and her friends, we will buy a home there and enjoy a happy marriage.

My new employees and I fight to take back the Flatbush streets. I give them better training, uniforms and weapons. The guards buff their new badges with pride.

My boyhood friends, out-of-work actresses, barflies and story-tellers, join us in our quest.

But some guards refuse to let go of old vices. Others turn vigilante and bully innocents.

Curbing their zeal, I try to teach them to uphold civil rights as I hunt the suspect in the comedian's murder.

Then, under cover of night, good and evil clash at the Lefferts Historic House. Facing disgrace and prison, I must decide what matters most in life to me.

Come walk with me on that razor edge between brutality and staying alive as Cooper and I, my Flippers and my guards give everything to try ***Softening Flatbush.***

Can Showbizzers Crush Crime?

Can I, Max Royster, fired from the NYPD for mental disease, on crutches, train a ragtag group of performers, my Showbizzers, to use their skills and bodies to stop a genius crime lord in the High Desert town of Basta, California?

§

Freezing, grieving my lost shield, I hobble aboard an Amtrak train. America passes by outside my window.

When we reach the California desert, my spirits rise. Hope for a new life makes me exit in the small sandy town of Basta.

The sun and beauty cheer me. But the town suffers from crime. A thug mugs me, taking my cash and ID.

That turns me sad again.

A group that I dub "My Showbizzers" – out-of-work dancers, actresses, dog trainers and writers – rescue me. They remind me of my live-for-the-moment cronies back in Manhattan, "The Playpen Irregulars." Thrilled by their energy, I fall in love with Koy, a beautiful Asian dog-handler.

Some Basta deputies duck work or bully innocents. Their sloppiness angers and frustrates me, and their laziness helps a local criminal genius, Crostwaite, rob a bank.

My Showbizzers have many skills. Maybe they could use those talents and creativity to fight crime. They might do better than some lazy deputies.

Nobody else believes in my idea. Locals mock me. The sheriff and the FBI block me. But I force myself to push my idea forward, while my Showbizzers must fight their own bias against government and rules.

But when Crostwaite starts killing, I train my Showbizzers. They go undercover. Their beautiful bodies use sex as a weapon. Koy trains dogs to burgle homes and seize evidence.

To avenge his childhood of horrors, Crostwaite vows to destroy Basta.

Frightened but passionate, without guns, power or respect, my Showbizzers and I risk everything to stop Crostwaite.

Our deadly showdown will answer the question once and for all: ***Can Showbizzers Crush Crime?***

When Max witnesses a debutante's kidnapping, he becomes the FBI's prime suspect. Or is he actually their salvation?

§

It's Christmas in Manhattan.

A blizzard whips the city.

The Beautiful People, in the elite Upper East Side, celebrate in their brownstones.

Until a kidnapper seizes a beautiful young debutante.

Max Royster, fired from the NYPD for mental illness, fights the kidnapper but loses.

The kidnapper flees. Stripped of gun, shield and power, Max has only his wits to save the victim.

The FBI treats Max like a suspect and tramples roughshod on his rights.

During this long sleepless night, an unknown FBI agent cracks up. Over the radio, he quotes J. Edgar Hoover and plants false clues.

To solve the case, Max must smash through the facade and mysteries of millionaires in their snug brownstones.

Exotic women tempt him to give up.

The blizzard worsens.

As the winds howl and snowdrifts deepen, Max risks his life and his freedom in a desperate bid to save the victim.

Once again, Max Royster is back on the street in *Brownstone Kidnap Crackup.*

To catch a sex killer targeting Upper East Side beauties, misfit NYPD cop Max Royster goes undercover…as an NYPD cop!

§

The Upper East Side of Manhattan is one of the richest neighborhoods in the world.

But Max Royster, a maverick, outspoken and erudite NYPD foot cop, who grew up working-class in this tony area, calls it "the Playpen." Money protects the bluebloods in this area like the bars on an infant's playpen.

Late one night, patrolling wealthy brownstones, he sees a burglar attacking a rich actress. Max chases him. They fight but the burglar escapes.

The burglar is a sexual predator, known in cop-speak as a "Horn Bug".

For losing the suspect, Max's captain deems Max "a Funny Bunny," too unstable for police work. He strips Max of his gun and badge, then orders Max into Bellevue Hospital for observation and maybe for the rest of his life.

Without any tools or support, Max has ten days to stop this Horn Bug.

The Gypsy Twist

Max Royster's hunt for a sadistic serial killer takes a startling turn when he realizes that not all predators are born alike.

§

One autumn night, someone strangles a teenage boy jogging in Central Park.

In Brooklyn, street cop Max Royster risks his life to disarm a madwoman with a knife without harming her. Nevertheless, her lawyer charges Max with brutality. The Department decides to punish Max.

Max's protector is Sgt. Lipkin, an expert detective working the Central Park murder. Lipkin knows that a killer like this seeks a new sexual thrill, a "Gypsy Twist," with each new murder. The dead boy is the son of one of the wealthy elite of the Upper East Side. Max is the only cop in the city from that world, and on scholarship years before, Max had even graduated from the dead boy's school.

Lipkin summons Max for the assistance that only Max can provide.

Max probes the tony school and neighborhood, ignoring bosses who, out of jealousy, try to block his progress.

A beautiful, free-spirited reporter, Diana, woos Max to try and make him reveal insights about the case. Denying him nothing, she lures Max onward.

The killer seizes another school-boy who was playing soccer in the park and drags him to death with a car.

Wealthy New Yorkers scream that someone is butchering their sons. The city rocks.

One night, muggers attack Sgt. Lipkin and Max, who freezes on the trigger. The muggers cripple Lipkin.

The Department moves to fire Max.

But the dead boy's tycoon father hires Max to track down the killer. Max and Diana live below the radar in the New Orleans and San Francisco underworlds, hunting the killer until a shocking conclusion reveals the killer's true identity.